Homage to the American Indians

Homage to

the American Indians

ERNESTO CARDENAL

translated by MONIQUE and CARLOS ALTSCHUL
illustrated by DINO ARANDA

The JOHNS HOPKINS UNIVERSITY PRESS Baltimore and London

Published in Spanish as *Homenaje a los Indios Americanos* © 1970 by Editorial Universitaria, S.A. Translation copyright © 1973 by The Johns Hopkins University Press

Photographs of original paintings by Dino Aranda reproduced by permission of the photographer, Taylor Gregg.

The Johns Hopkins University Press, Baltimore, Maryland 21218
The Johns Hopkins University Press Ltd., London

Library of Congress Catalog Card Number 73-8111
ISBN 0-8018-1513-4 (clothbound edition)
ISBN 0-8018-1514-2 (paperbound edition)

Originally published, 1973
Johns Hopkins Paperbacks edition, 1973

Library of Congress Cataloging in Publication Data will be found on the last printed page of this book.

CONTENTS

Homage to the American Indians

Ball Player

NELE OF KANTULE

NELE OF KANTULE:
                         model of statesmen and presidents
                    Yes, model of American Presidents
                    Every year on the anniversary of his death
there are dances on the island of Ustupo
Hero of the native revolt against
                         the *waga* (foreigners) in 1925
               After the revolt
schools were established at Tigre
                    Ustupo, Ailigandi
                    Tikantiki, Tuipile, Playon Chico
          with Indian teachers
He created the Library at Ustupo, under the coconut trees
                         the NELE OF KANTULE Library
He bought a steamer for his village in 1931
the steamer *Esfera*
He signed agreements with General Preston Brown
on the labor of the Indians in the Canal Zone
treaties with the President of Panama
He defended his people from the Panamanian police
He obtained scholarships for Indians
at the School of Arts and at the National Institute

In 1932 he introduced voting booths
        and requested increases in school personnel.
NELE OF KANTULE
by seeing only the seed he could describe the entire plant
He knew all the traditions and the sacred songs
He was no friend of civilization
                            indiscriminately accepted
nor of extremely traditional views
        of rejecting everything from the *waga* but:
of assimilating the benefits of civilization
yet retaining all those traditions treasured by the indians
When he brought in civilization
                        he began by teaching himself first
Scholarships were meant to prepare his people
as teachers, craftsmen, agrarian experts
        He did not desire political power
                        only to serve his people.
At 10 he used to go after plants with his father
to the river banks and the islands
At 12 he began to describe his dreams
At 17 he went to the Caiman River in Colombia
to study with Inayoga, the old Nele
First: the behavior necessary to become a Nele:
"Know how to be gracious to others
                    and not to be proud"
Afterwards, the ancient history of the islands, the
famous Neles of San Blas:
Nesquesura, who taught how to bury the dead
            not to have intercourse before the eyes of others
He had arrived when men were in chaos, Nesquesura
            who preached the word from village to village
Magus (another great man) spoke of murder
Cupna talked about friendship
and about giving to the hungry and to the thirsty
Tuna taught men to build hammocks

Sue, knower of natural phenomena
taught that all manner of fruits exist
He spoke of the rivers *Olopurgandihual, Manipurgandihual,*
                    Siapurgandihual and *Calipurgandihual*
Men did not know how to share the fruits
and Mr. Sue said they were to be harvested in an orderly way
          Men stole from one another
and that is why the wind blew stronger than before
                    Mr. Sue would explain.
Tequenteba was an engineer and a knower of foods:
          jonny, rolls, foods with yucca
Spoke of sharing the plantations
Ibelele told of the words of God
he said the enemies were:
Masalaiban (the anteater) and *Masolototobaliel* (the iguana)
          who do not believe in God.
These Neles were great doctors
sent by God. They have been very wise
     knew all the medicines
called the leopards, tigerlings and jaguars to their homes
to chat with them
               They could calm the great hurricanes
The wild fishes were friends to the Neles
and these Neles would call assemblies to sing to the people
while the great winds began to blow.
          Tiegun explored the world of the evil spirits
and talked about them
          Sibu visited the region of the dead
Salupip explained how God had created different kinds of animals.
And above all the Neles, Ibeorgun
two years after *Mu-osis* (the Flood)
                         came Ibeorgun
he came to teach them to greet, to tell them
                         that it is good to greet
                    that it is to think about God
                         to give good greetings

3

he showed them the tobacco plant and told them it was called *huar*
"I call tobacco *huar*"
and when it is to be smoked or if it will be used as incense
                    it is to be named *tola*
                (and they did not understand)
He was the first man to come to give names to the Cunas
At sunbreak he held a meeting with the people
And said, God has sent me to teach here on earth
and told them to learn the songs
Absogeti-Igala, Camu-Igala, Caburri-Igala, etc.
                    the medicine songs
which God said they should learn
            This came from the mouth of God
                    and we must learn it here on earth
And as in those times men did not know how to say brother
he told them that for brother they were to say *Carguenatdi*
and for sister *Om*
to name the husband of my aunt it is said *Tuc-so*
and the husband of the sister of the wife is *Ambe-suhi*
and the brother or sister of the father-in-law is called *Saca*
and he told them to say that above in the sky is God
and we call him *Diosayla* (Dad)
and Ibeorgun said that the land in which God has left us
we call *Nap-cu-na*
for we are in the center of the world
            we are in *Kuna*
He told them we are on the surface of the earth
and we walk upright, *ucurmacque* that is:
                "we walk on earth"
He taught them the four kinds of thread to make shirts with
and the juices of the plants to dye them with bright colors
and the four kinds of clay for pots
and thus also do people have different colors of skin
He invented the use of gold for dishes and spoons, and for
the nose pendants of women

4

that is why women still wear
                            rings in their noses.
And Nele of Kantule learned medicine with Inayoga
the useful plant and the useless one
                how to cut them, the
prayers each plant had
the bark of the *baila-ukka* is for headaches
the lizard's butter for the flu
                coca calms pain
the *utirbe* palm tree strengthens the body
the *yerba de culebra* (snake herb) is for snake bites
and he learned which
                            tree is good for wounds
the leaf for eye rinsing and for sketching
the bejuco to learn languages
the medicine against drunkenness
and the medicine to be humble
            the trunk, spotted like a snake, to
                            cure shyness with the wife
                the root to cure madness.
And from there he went to Arquia (Colombia)
                            where the master Orwity lived
            to learn the history of the ancient *caciques*
because he knew that some day he'd be the *Cacique* of the islands
                Orwity
            was the one who knew the history of the *caciques* the best
                and had 20 students who would be neles
        the teaching of the *caciques* lasted 3 years
and Nele of Kantule began to speak at Meetings
Later he wanted to know modern civilization
and went to Quibdo (Colombia)
where the Indian master Jesus Manuel lived
                who finished his schooling in Cartagena
            And spent three more years with him
And to learn the culture of Europe he went to Socupti (Panama)

where the Indian master William Smith, who had been a sailor, lived
              and who had sailed throughout Europe
and he studied with him one more year.
                    His studies finished, the teacher said
that if he wished to know about the American nations
       he should go to Charles Aspinwal who lived in Acandi
         And Nele went to the little village of Acandi,
                         Colombia
lovely Acandi comes to my mind! I was there:
In the mouth of a river and by the sea, with coconut trees . . .
       And in the hut of Aspinwal, under the coconut trees
surely, by the
sea, he received his "education on the American nations
and on the Independence
                 and on the life of the Liberator Simon Bolivar
       and on the names of all his generals and battles"
There he studied one more year.
Finally he went to the village of Paya (Panama)
                         where the master Nitipilele lived
         to learn further about the Cuna language
because this master knew how the names of all things
                              that are on earth
              had come about
and there he studied two more years.
At that time Nele of Kantule returned
to Portogandi, his village, ready
to rule. Portogandi had just been flooded by the river
         only 6 huts remained
and he ordered the village to be taken to an island (to Ustupo)
This was in 1903, and on that island he began
                         his political career.
              They made him *cacique*
         —Inapaguina was the *Great Cacique*—
His first two tasks:
         to promote agriculture

and good will to the other *caciques* of the islands
Two teachers he took to Ustupo:
                         a Spanish teacher and an English teacher
Charlie Robinson, the famous *cacique* Robinson, wanted
no part of the ancient history of the forefathers
                    only Spanish history
These were their differences
Because Nele said:
                "our history is important"
Later Colman was the *Great Cacique*, Simral
Colman, the great Colman
he who said: "I want you to love one another
that you not kill like animals the people
                              who have the same faces
hair and blood
and that you love also those who belong to other races
as well as your enemies"
and in another speech:
                "We must defend our gold mines
our iron and lead mines
and all the metals that are in the earth
and the fishes that are in the sea
and even the insects"
         And Colman named Nele *Sub-Cacique* (1923)
      and afterwards called an assembly
so that he be acknowledged *Great Cacique* of all San Blas
And Nele of Kantule became the Nele par excellence
they called him simply Nele
                    or Dr. Nele
He knew the Cuna traditions
              better than any other Nele of San Blas
The good things of civilization have to be accepted he used to say
            without forgetting the Cuna traditions
He was "a knower of the world of dreams"
He dictated the *History of the Cuna Indians* to his secretaries

He asked that the most interesting books be read to him
He worked in the community's chicken pen
                              when his turn came
He wrote prayers for his people: "Father, I want to sleep now
        Father, lower the net of gold and pearls
            between diseases and me
                Father, lower the mosquito net of silver and pearls
                between disease and me"
He cured with songs and with magical herbs
            yet also with penicillin from the Canal Zone
He scolded parents if
                    their children did not go to school
And the last words of the Cacique to his people were:
"10 days after my death you shall call an assembly
to acknowledge the Great Chief who will succeed me
I recommend Mr. Olotebiliguina who was the leader
of the 1925 revolt for *Great Cacique*
Let him continue my relationships with the Panamanian Government
let him gather those that speak Spanish by his side
or those who are interpreters of the Cuna language
Let Law #59 of the Indian Reservation be respected
And all the *caciques* of San Blas are to unite
as one man they are to unite
to defend the rights of the coconut and its price."
And before dying he was baptized.
The missionary asked him if he believed in God
            and he answered:
                                "He is"
—"I wish you to see God"
            —"I am seeing God my Father"
    Nele of Kantule is buried surrounded by the waters of wonders
where the Indians fish
        on a churchyard-island by the island of Ustupo
And he is now seeing the vision of God.

That small coral island is a heavenly churchyard
Green and blue water
                              and the coral at the bottom . . .
Blossoming skeletons that grow under the water
(green where it is shallow and blue where it is deeper)
like figures of the resurrection. The coconut trees sing like Neles
like Neles singing in Cuna
And if one flies by on a plane
                                        one may see the long sunken net
—the very long fishing net—
                              and will see the bottom!

Every year in his honor
there are dances in Ustupo.

LOST CITIES

At night owls fly between the stelae,
the mountain lion meows on the terraces,
the jaguar roars in the towers
and the lone coyote barks in the Grand Plaza
to the reflection of the moon in the lakes
that once were ponds in distant katuns.

The stylized animals
on the frescoes are now real
and the princes sell clay pots in the markets.
But how to write anew the hieroglyph,
how to paint the jaguar anew, how to overthrow the tyrants?
How to build our tropical acropolises anew,
our country seats surrounded by milpas?

The underbrush is full of monuments.
There are altars in the milpas.
Among the roots of the *chilamates,* arches with reliefs,
in the forest where one would think no man has ever trod,
where only the tapir and the lone-coati enter

and the quetzal is still dressed as a Maya:
there is a metropolis there.
When the priests climbed the Temple of the Jaguar
with cloaks of jaguar and fans of quetzal tails
and sandals of deer leather and ritual masks,
screams rose from the Ball Game,
the sound of drums, the incense of *copal* burning
in the holy chambers lined with sapota wood,
smoke of *ocote* torches . . . and under Tikal
there is another metropolis, a thousand years older.
—Where monkeys now howl in the *sapota* trees.

There are no names of soldiers on the stelae.

In their temples and palaces and pyramids
and in their calendars and chronicles and codices
there are no names of caudillos caciques emperors
nor of priest leader statesman general or chief
and they did not record political events on their stones
nor administrations, nor dynasties,
nor ruling families, nor political parties.
For centuries you cannot find the glyph of a man's name
and archeologists still don't know how they used to rule themselves!

The word "Lord" was foreign to the tongue.
And the word "wall." They did not wall in their cities.
Their cities were of temples and they lived in the fields,
among milpas and palm and papaya trees.
The arch of their temples was a copy of their huts.
The roads were only for processions.
Religion was the only tie among them,
but it was a religion freely taken
and neither an oppression nor a burden on them.

Their priests had no earthly power
and their pyramids were built without forced labor.
The peak of their civilization did not lead to an empire.
And they had no colonies. They did not know the arrow.
They knew Jesus as the god of corn
and they offered him simple sacrifices
of corn and birds and feathers.
They had no wars nor knew the wheel
but calculated the synodic revolution of Venus:
every evening they took note of the ascent of Venus
in the horizon, on a distant ceiba tree,
when the couples of *lapa* birds flew back to their nests.
They did not work metals. Their tools were of stone,
and technologically they remained in the Stone Age.
But they computed exact dates that were
400 million years ago.
They did not develop applied sciences. They were not practical.
Their progress took place in religion, in the arts, in mathematics,
in astronomy. They did not know how to weigh.
They worshipped time, that mysterious flowing
and flowing of time.
Time was sacred. The days were gods
Past and future suffused their songs.
They counted past and future with the same katuns
because they believed time repeats itself
as they saw the rotation of the stars repeat itself
But the time they worshipped stopped suddenly.

There are stelae that were not engraved.
The blocks remained half-cut in the quarries.
—And they are still there.—

Now only the solitary chicle-hunters cross the Peten.
Vampires nest in the stucco friezes

Wild pigs grunt in the evening.
The jaguar roars in the towers—the towers among the roots—
a coyote, far, on a square barks to the moon,
and a plane of the Pan American Airlines flies over the pyramid.
But will the past katuns ever come back?

MEXICAN SONGS I

The quetzal feathers dry
the mosaics of hummingbird feathers bleach like flowers
the mosaics of turquoise, jade, obsidian and mother-of-pearl
fall like flowers.
Necklaces of snails and jade scatter
              like strings of cacao flowers . . .

The white vases, like codex sheets,
             with designs in light red and dark red
      yellow
           and turquoise green
vases of red clay like red *chiles*
vases of red clay of Oaxaca like ripe fruits
or as orange as fire
             wilt and crack.
     If it is a pyramid
it crumbles.

Quetzal feathers turn pale
            and are full of dust!

Hear the lamentations that I, King Netzahualcoyotl, utter
The universe is a ball game
in it we play with two balls: the Sun and the Moon
against the powers of hell
and we do not know who will win (whoever loses shall die)
And see the sign of the Sun in the center of the Calendar
    —the sign of the Sun is in the center—
in the morning it is *Tonatiuh* ("the ascending Eagle")
because it is like an eagle which rises to the nopal in the morning
squeezing the red tunas of the human hearts
and it is *Cuauhtemoc* in the afternoon
            ("the descending Eagle")
The rubber ball goes up and down, and comes and goes
and we men have to play with this ball.
Death and life: black and red ink
double ink with which the poets paint their codices.

The lake of Texcoco and Tenochtitlan
           ("the lake of the moon")
which is like a mirror of obsidian in the moonlight
and in the sunlight, greenish blue
         of quiet turquoise
    emerald and gold
lake of waters of flowers, where the duck swims
and comes and goes swimming
and flies cawing and moving its tail full of sun
it will also dry up one day like the flowers.
The lake of Texcoco and Tenochtitlan ("the lake of the moon")
will be like a dream we had on a moonlit night.
And that fades in the morning.
       And in its place will rise clouds of dust.

That is why my song is sad
and the *teponaztli* keeps its sad beat.
Do not ask why the *teponaztli* sounds so sad!

We only come to earth to dream
to leave some illuminated manuscripts
$$\text{like dreams.}$$
The pottery of the Toltecs lies under the earth
strewn like flower petals.
We have painted the inside of the sky on deer skin
but will our descendants understand the Codex?

Our poems on maguey, yucca and palm paper
will be carried by the wind like the dust of Texcoco.

Those who saw the court of the old king Tezozomoc
the tyrant:
and saw the dancers dressed as tigers and birds
and the *huehuetl* players crowned with flowers
and the gardens resounding with the timbrel of their fountains
would now only see this pile of stones
where the *tecolote* sings to death.
He oppressed the weak, the humble, the *macehuales*
that carry lumber in the mountain and hunt for maguey
and now the *macehual* finds his lumber and his maguey
in the ditches and baths of the powerful king Tezozomoc.

The reigns of kings are brief as roses.
What became of the princes dressed with quetzal feathers
and the princesses with eyes of obsidian?
Look for them in the royal vases
$$\text{which you will find full of dust.}$$
They have gone like the smoke of Popocatepetl . . .
They are only shadows from Mictlan, the Region of Mystery.
$$\text{Do not wonder if the *teponaztli* sounds so sad}$$
$$\text{I Netzahualcoyotl}$$
will soon be in my pot of clay, at one with the mud

(a few bones with necklaces)
I was made of clay like a vessel
                    a vessel of clay that returns to the clay
and the King of Texcoco will be the equal of any *macehual.*

But look at the Sun: it is reborn every day from Mictlan, the Region
                            of the Dead
and Quetzalcoatl the morning star dies and is reborn
                See how Quetzalcoatl shines in the morning!
See the corn: it dies and
is reborn tender after the first rains sent by Tlaloc.
If there isn't but dust in the pot
it is because mother Cihuacoatl is grinding me as on a grindstone
and my blossoming bones will revive!
Quetzalcoatl will take me from Mictlan.
Nobody can alter this Codex of black and red ink,
the paintings that sing of the One for whom all live
                the Master of the near and the together.

MEXICAN SONGS II

I have not come to make wars on earth
but to pick flowers
I am the singer-king who looks for flowers
                              I, Netzahualcoyotl
my palace is full of singers
                    not of soldiers.

Picker of cacao flowers . . .
Not Cacaos (the COINS
for buying and selling in markets, and not for drinking)
            but the flower.
Let millionaires treasure their cacaos, let dictators
            treasure their *xiquipiles* of cacaos
        and I the flowers.
My valuable flowers.
Gentlemen,
the cacao flower is more valuable than the cacao.

I pick the flowers of friendship. Flowers
of love, Dictators!
                Flowers of song.

And in the song I look only for Friendship, the meeting
of the singers. Literary Competitions
under flower groves.
> *Xiquipiles* of songs.
> *Xiquipiles* of flowers.
I yearn for the Brotherhood, the Nobility
of the poets.
> The "Association"
Mine is a court of singers.
> Gentlemen Generals and Tigers
my court is gloomy and of kettle-drums.
> And I do not ORDER.
I, "Yoyontzin" (King Netzahualcoyotl)
> am always singing.

My song is of friendship, brothers.
Only in flowers is there a Brotherhood.
Embraces
> only in the flowers.

The federation of poet friends are those flowers. The meeting
> of friends.
This poem is a flower.
> I sing of that brotherhood.

But the cacao flowers dry up.
The singer comes from heaven
Flowers and songs from the inside of heaven
yes, from its Inside. Flowers sprout, flowers sprout
from my kettle-drum. Flower-Song are my words.
I always sing. I do not meddle
> with Propaganda
You are in these songs Giver of Life.
I give my flowers and songs to my people.
> —I sow poems, not tributes.
Do not let me sing in vain.

We have come to bring joy to Anahuac with paintings
The flowers of painting
                        —those of the books
             Songs painted in the books.
And the paintings of the Region of Mystery
                  "that which is over us."
There
        where our songs were born . . .

            Are these the flowers of the Giver of Life?
No. Your flowers are not these.
            Where will I see your flowers?
I, poet, search for You
and am sad.
            I, "Yoyontzin"
will see you one day.
Friendship, like the pink cacao flower, withers.
And like the milk flower of the *zacuanjoche.*
Things are flowers, they wither.
And I do not tire of flowers.
We are not happy.
        Many flowers
                 and my heart isn't full
Did we ever feel delight in life? Delight
even for a moment?
Send me to the Meeting,
to the region where our people gather!

There,
      "where all unite"
                there is friendship there!
We look for your flowers and your songs, Giver of Life.
        We can always find kettle-drums there.

I sing with weeping.
The Region from where song comes! The Region
of the Meeting. My heart
saddens . . . Your songs
Giver of Life, are more beautiful
than the golden necklace the archeologist unearths
              or the fan of quetzal wilting in the Museum.
I dress with songs as with a quetzal cloak

The night wind is casting flowers.
Who dances to the drums? It is I, "Yoyontzin"
—Ministers, Presidents, Gentlemen—
                    the King who dances to the drums.

Do not let me sing in vain.

Non-Mayan Mayapan

MAYAPAN

The Carnegie Institution of Washington, D.C.
            finds everything together in Uaxactun
stelae with hieroglyphs polychrome ceramics stone temples
    everything appears simultaneously
                                        Uaxactun
before the first date (Stela #9)
April 328 A.D. says the almost erased hieroglyph (Stela #9)
still standing, 17 centuries later, as Morley found it.
Stela #10: glyphs erased beyond
deciphering.
Sixth-century erection of stelae
            in Tulum, in Ichpaahtun (on the coast of Yucatan)
    Lacanha in the woods of Chiapas, South of the Usumacinta
                Pusilha (British Honduras)
                    (who gives a damn for these names)
everywhere erection of stelae erection of stelae
and later fewer stelae
                in some cities there are no more stelae
Tikal and Uaxactun: no more stelae
and later another Renaissance ("Classical Period")
the shape of the vessel changes and the drawings on them
the architecture changes
            the profiles in the stelae have turned around

not one foot any more (hiding the other)
but the body facing forward and both feet facing forward
only the head in profile (neck gently bent
into the stone)
the stone of the façades carved better
An unknown artist in his studio
                    bent searching for other lines
another style, *avant garde*
poets with new isms
                Mayan isms
creating
            another stage of civilization for the Mayas
and from city unto city the fever of stelae, the
            new wave of stelae
                    the school of stelae
holy
skyscrapers, in the forest
                   mystic skyscrapers
—If I could
          fly again to Tikal
in an airplane—
"artificial volcanoes" they said
and Tikal full of stelae, hieroglyphs
well-carved texts
              Calakmul, more stelae than Tikal
        Palenque
           Copan
               Yaxchilan
well-carved texts on the altars on the lintels
    texts   texts
long texts
            texts on the steps
long texts climbing the long line of steps
the meticulously carved poem on the stone stairs
toward the sky

It happened
            at the time of the Honduran astronomers . . .
The line in Yaxchilan and Copan was more delicate
                  the details of the jewels
on the suit, the grains of the ear of corn, the hairdo, clearer
the hieroglyph loaded with meaning (of old masters)
looser the movement of the dance
on the stone.
At the time of the Astronomers' Meeting in Honduras . . .
Over the tropical forest: the *skyline** of Tikal, and
not far from there, as for example in New Jersey
                              another *skyline**
"*Building Boom*"* in Guatemala and
            "*Stela Boom*"*
Cities? Yes
            but sacred cities
        not Commercial Centers
but ceremonial centers
rows of stelae and stelae, not
                        neon, not commercial ads
(their ads: poems on stones!)
Those rooms are dark: cells
for prayer and fasting
Novices . . . sleepless nights
                  Tikal white in the moonlight
or in the long rainy nights . . .
O Tikal white in the sun!
        darkness inside
and down there the screams of the sacred base-ball.
What did the tourist see?
Pyramid after pyramid temple after temple
                  ("when the Pyramids were white . . .")
façades facing the sun
stairs under the sun in light and shade
each step half light half shade

*In English in the original.

temples white or in the shade, lights and shadows
a dark wall and the other side in the light
                white and black
white and black in the green
and some taller than others, pyramids beyond pyramids
here from the central square
of Tikal, as where Broadway and 42d. Street meet
DISSOLVE . . . .
Broken stairways
                gray against the sky
        faded by time
monkeys on the trees that cover them
                rubber trees, chicle trees
Now the camera pans on:
debris embraced by the *mata-palo*
lianas
        thick as fire-hoses

. . . to fly again to Tikal
in an airplane. To fly over Ciudad Flores
which is in the middle of the lake.

Roads were not for cars
                but for rituals
roads, religious
Cities had no defenses
                (like today's little Mayan towns, defenseless
                among its milpas)
They had neither walls nor barracks
        the word "wall" does not exist in their language
        the word "barracks" does not exist in their language
So democratic
        that archeologists know nothing about their rulers

I said that before (Classical Period)
Now I'm not interested in it. The Cocoms interest me
the Cocom family ("Vine of yellow flowers")
              that is, *mata-palo*
                  and Mayapan "THE WALLED CITY"
Non-Mayan Mayapan
". . . because of the treason of Hunaac Ceel ruler of Mayapan . . ."
Unearthed in Mayapan
                          —Carnegie Institution of Washington, D.C.
the cultural poverty of that military regime!
Centralization in Mayapan. Totalitarianism. Control over Yucatan.
Those huge ruins (around them, a wall) few temples
many palaces
few hieroglyphs in Chichen
and fewer texts yet in Mayapan
Dictatorship. The mediocre temple of Kukulkan
mediocre temples (copies)
Great stone façades, naked stone
coarsely carved
The columns aren't worth a shit
Monochrome pottery, monotonous
as at the beginning, as the Olmecs
or: as filling station billboards on a Texas highway
No jewels at the burials
for the Beyond, only skulls
no beautiful object for those chiefs for the Beyond
but prisoners, but slaves, and plenty of food (in cheap pots)
Mass executions for their Beyond.
Chichen Itza already decayed
                  the Snail Tower crumbling
That due to the triumph of Hunaac Ceel
(The pottery tells it)
              (1200 A.D. according to the pottery)
          and after that no more pottery.

Because of the treason
                    ("because of the sin of word of Hunaceel"
                                        says the Chumayel)
And metal appears in Mayapan. I repeat
metal appears. And the exiles
o the exiled men of Chichen Itza!
                    "I was a tender child
                                in Chichen
                    when the evil man
                                the Master of the Army
        came to snatch the land
        O atheism was born
                    in Chichen Itza."
The imported bow and arrow
                                they did not know them before
                                They were not invented there
The best masonry
            for the houses of the noblemen not for the temples
Good sculpture (Puuc style) (i.e. Antiques)
in the house of the rich
Mediocre sculptures in the temples
(censers of bad, porous clay; and made in molds;
gods by the tens, *mass production, assembly line,** Henry Ford.
Technical advances, no doubt
and after the entire dynasty of the Hunaac Ceel, the Cocoms
250 years in power those Cocoms
Cocom, which in Maya means:
"Vine of yellow flowers, Somoza family, *mata-palo*."
Aztecs the *Ah Canul* (bodyguards)
and the Cocoms selling the Mayas
selling Mayas to foreigners
    ". . . . and that he so brought Mexican people to Mayapan, that
            Cocom was the first in making slaves . . ."
Until Ah Xupan rebelled.

*In English in the original.

28

The rebellion triumphed.
All the Cocoms murdered
no, with the exception of one, the kid who was in Honduras or wherever
Large amounts of coal, scorched rafters among debris,
there is the rebellion unearthed by Carnegie. And skulls,
obsidian between the ribs; in a pelvis . . .
But pyramids
                were not built any more

        Mayapan fell!
                        Mayapan fell!
        The walled Mayapan fell!
                        The green bird, the comforter
                        green quetzal on the green branch
                        announces dawn
                        with the Morning Star, he who awakes
                        and the *chachalaca-face-of-sun*
                        the town's watchbird, peals
                        peals announcing the sun.
        MAYAPAN THE WALLED CITY FELL

But pyramids were not built any more
for temples, palm huts
the roads were not repaired
                civil wars since then
The *mata-palo* in the pyramid, crumbling it . . .
And prophet-poets prophetizing bad *katuns*
        13 Ahau: "no more lucky days for us"
        11 Ahau: "the katun is a miser; the rains scarce . . . misery"
         7 Ahau: "carnal sin, gangsters in the government"
         5 Ahau: "evil his face, evil news"
        10 Ahau: "drought is the weight of this katun"
And no more cult to Quetzalcoatl
                —current Mayas

*In English in the original.

do not remember Quetzalcoatl—
Artcrafts of Guatemala, what's left of that art
fabrics for tourists, Mexican curios
    the snapshot is gloomy
it is a color snapshot but it is gloomy
*Colorful**
    (That
        toucan I saw in Tikal
by the hotel . . .)
        The military are to blame
Non-Mayan Mayapan
And
    like someone coming down a pyramid
                (1200-1450 A.D.)
      the loss of Mayan values
from a tall pyramid
        down to the forest

Time Time Time
those stelae had been
concerned with the mystery of time
or: obsession with eternity
Dates, backward,
          looking for eternity
looking for the future also
backward, into eternity
Each time further backward
the calendar of a year Ninety Million years ago
    (in Quirigua, Honduras)
and Four Hundred Million years ago
      (right there, Quirigua, on another stela)
and even further back!
The progress of astronomy and mathematics on those stones
progress of the astronomer-priests priest-scientists

*In English in the original.

and the best engraving artists, the
          figure of "god," well drawn
But backward progress
                    each time further back
until the beginning of time (or was there no beginning???)
through the Past
                    like opening a causeway in the forest
of an infinite Peten!
To the beginning when everything was in suspense
everything motionless
                                        everything silent
          everything empty
     only alone quiet the sea the sky all
and nothing gathered   nothing noisy
          and everything was invisible   everything
                                   motionless in heaven
     only the water quiet   only
          the sea peaceful
               and nothing existed that existed
only immovability   the silence
     in the darkness
                    in the night
only the Heart of Heaven
                    Hurricane its name

The Cosmos a milpa
and the invention of the gigantic calendar
          of 374,440 years
                    was for the great milpa
or better:
          universal immortality
Its astronomy religion of infinite
and the construction of pyramids on pyramids
the ancient pyramid under the new

on old structures, taller ones superimposed
　　　　—the pyramid #E-VII
　　　　　　　under pyramid #VIIa of group E—
　　with hopes for eternity:
until, the milpa once harvested
and the Great Calendar achieved,
everything would be again
　　　　　　　　in peace　　　　　　silence
　　　　only immovability　　　　　　　　silence
only the Heart of Heaven
　　　　　　　　　　　　Hurricane its name

But time is circular it repeats itself
past present future are the same
revolutions of the sun
　　　　　　　　revolutions of the moon
synodic revolutions of the planets
and history also revolutions
They repeat themselves
And the priests
　　　　　　keeping track
　　　　　　　　calculating
the revolutions
And every 260 years (a Year of years)
history repeats itself. The katuns repeat themselves
Past katuns are those of the future
history and prophecy are the same

The Katun 8 Ahau was one of struggle
　　　　　　　　　　and political change
and each time the 8 Ahau would return
　　　　　　there would be struggle and political change

32

In the Katun 8 Ahau *"Mayapan fell"*
                    (so says the CHILAM BALAM OF CHUMAYEL)
... *"To empty the city of Mayapan*
                              of the power gathered in it ..."
The Ides of March of the Mayas!
Katun 8 Ahau:
                    ... *"It will be the end of their greed*
the end of the suffering they cause to the world ..."
                                        (CHILAM BALAM)
... *"When the hour of all those who ruled arrives ...*
                    ... of all the sons of bitches ...
... *this is the word of the 8 Katun Ahau*
              the same in which Mayapan was depopulated ...
... *bad is the word of the Katun but it will happen thus ..."*
                                        (CHILAM BALAM)
Katun 8 Ahau:
... *"The hasty snatching of purses will come*
and the quick and violent war of the greedy thieves:
this is the burden of the Katun for Christian times ..."
                                        (CHILAM BALAM)
and (the terrible words of the Chumayel, Book X):
... *"It is not necessary for you to give your head*
                              to the Archbishop
              ... they are now with the Cocoms ..."

          ... *"It will be the end of oppression and unhappiness for all*
              It is the word of God ..."
                                        (CHILAM BALAM)
And I therefore say that Mayapan will fall
          Mayapan the walled city always falls in this katun

              Mayan rubber for Goodyear
              Mayan chicle for Adams Chiclets

The military are to blame, and now
on the palm wall the calendar of CARLOS OCHOMOGO & BROS.
                              pin-up whore combing her hair
        "General Stores——Best Prices in Town"
(and the Bristol Calendar)
and in the town's movie theater Dorothy Lamour
                              tickets: 50 quetzal cents
on a par with the dollar
The snake-tailed quetzal, Quetzalcoatl-quetzal
on a par with the dollar?
                              It neither lives in captivity
nor is it a coin, shitty *quetzal*
It lives free in the forests
(I saw a quetzal on the large desk
of President Arevalo
                    but it was stuffed)
it flies green in the forest
              And there is hope
"Nobody covets more than what is fair
          (about the current Mayas)
          because they know it would be
                    at somebody else's expense"
and also:
"money plays a small part
          in the Mayan economy"
                              —Thompson says

1200-1450 A.D.
              This is the
                 Ste
                  la

34

THE ECONOMY OF TAHUANTINSUYU

They had no currency
    gold was used to fashion the lizard
    and NOT COINS
           the garments
               which flashed like fire
       in the light of the sun or of the bonfires
the images of the gods
          and the women they had loved
and not coins
      Millions of forges shining in the night of the Andes
and a bounty of gold and silver
        they had no money
they knew how
            to cast roll weld carve
gold and silver
    gold: sweat of the sun
        silver: tears of the moon
    Threads beads filigrane
              pins
              pectorals
              jingle bells

but not MONEY
and because there was no money
there was neither prostitution nor plunder
the doors of the houses stayed open
there was no Administrative Graft nor embezzlement
—every 2 years
they reported to Cuzco
because there was no commerce no money
there was no
sale of Indians
No Indian was ever sold
and there was *chicha* for everybody

They did not know the inflationary power of money
Their coin was the Sun which shines for everybody
the Sun that belongs to everybody and makes everything grow
the Sun without inflation and deflation: and not
those dirty "soles" with which the *peon* is paid
(who will show you his ruins for a Peruvian *sol*)
And they ate twice a day throughout the Empire

Financiers were not
the creators of their myths

Later the gold was stolen from the temples of the Sun
and went into circulation in ingots
with Pizarro's initials
Money brought taxes
and the first beggars appeared with the Colony

The water sings no longer in the stone channels
the roads are torn

lands dry as mummies
                        as mummies
of happy girls who danced
in *Airiway* (April)
                        the month of the Dance of the Sweet Corn
now dry and squatting in Museums

Manco Capac! Manco Capac!
                        Rich in virtues and not in money
(Mancjo: "virtue," Capacj: "rich")
"Man rich in virtues"
A system of economics without CURRENCY
the moneyless society we dream of
They valued gold just
as they valued the pink marble or the grass
and they offered it as food
                        like grass
            to the horses of the conquerors
upon seeing them chew metal (the bridles)
                        with their foamy mouths
They did not have money
and nobody starved in their whole Empire
and the dye of their *ponchos* has lasted 1,000 years
even princesses spun on their spindles
the blind shelled corn
children hunted birds
KEEP THE INDIANS BUSY
                        was an Inca slogan
the lame the maimed the old worked
        there were neither lazy nor idle men
whoever could not work would be fed
and the Inca worked painting and drawing
When the Empire fell

                    the Indian squatted
like a pile of ashes
and has done nothing but think . . .
                    indifferent to skyscrapers
        to the Alliance for Progress
                To think? Who knows
The architect of Macchu Picchu
in houses of cardboard
                            and Quaker Oats boxes
The carver of emeralds, hungry and smelly
        (the tourist takes a snapshot)
Lonely as a cactus
as silent as the landscape—in the background—of the Andes
                    They are ashes
        they are ashes
that the wind of the Andes fans
And the crying llama loaded with kindling
silently stares at the tourist
close to its owners

They did not have money
                Nobody was ever sold
And they did not exploit the miners
the extraction of mercury with snake movements
                (which caused the Indians to tremble)
was FORBIDDEN
The fishing of pearls was forbidden
And the Army was not hated by the people
The function of the State
                            was to feed the people
The land belonged to whoever worked it
                    and not to the landlord
And the Pleiades watched over the cornfields

There was land for all
                Free water and guano
        (there was no guano monopoly)
Compulsory banquets for the people
And when work started each new year
the plots were distributed with songs and *chicha*
                and to the beat of the drum of tapir hide
                and to the sound of the flute of jaguar bone
the Inca plowed the first furrow with his golden plow
Even the mummies took along their pouch of grain
for the trip to the Beyond

There was protection for domestic animals
llamas and vicuñas were covered by legislation
even the animals of the jungle had their code
                (which now the Sons of the Sun do not have)

4 causeways began
        at the Plaza de la Alegria in Cuzco
                        (the center of the world)
toward the 4 regions in which the Empire was divided
        "The Four Horizons"
    TAHUANTINSUYU
                        And the hanging bridges
over roaring rivers
                        paved highways
little winding roads in the hills
everything converged
                at the Plaza de la Alegria in Cuzco
                the center of the world

The heir to the throne
                followed his father to the throne
                        BUT NOT TO HIS POSSESSIONS

Agrarian communism?
Agrarian communism
                    "THE SOCIALIST EMPIRE OF THE INCAS"
Neruda: there was no freedom
                            but social security
And not everything was perfect at the "Inca Paradise"
They censured history, as told by knots
Free motels on the roads
                    without freedom to travel
And the purges of Atahualpa?
                            The scream of the exile
in the Amazonian forest?
                        The Inca was God
                                was Stalin

        (No opposition was tolerated)
Singers only sang the official history
Amaru Tupac was erased from the list of kings

But their myths
                were not those of the Economists!
Religious truth
                and political truth
were one and the same to the people
Economics *with* religion
                the lands of the Inca were the last to be plowed
first those of the Sun (those of the Church)
followed by those of the widows and orphans
followed by those of the people
                and the fields of the Inca plowed last

An Empire of *ayllus*
                    ayllus of working families
fauna flora minerals
            also divided in *ayllus*
the entire universe one great *ayllu*

40

(and today instead of the *ayllu*: latifundia)
The land could not be taken
Llacta mama (the soil) belonged to all
        Mother of all

Harvests were collected with songs and *chicha*
today there is panic at the Stock Exchange due to good harvests
                —the Ghost of Abundance—
A.P., NEW YORK,
                  (on the long strip of yellow paper)
SUGAR FUTURES MARKET DOWN TODAY
SALES AFFECTED BY PRICE DECREASE
IN EXPORT MARKET AND BY PREDICTED
RECORD WORLD HARVEST
the Phantom of Peace
            also shakes the Stock Exchange
the teletype trembles
THE STOCK EXCHANGE SUFFERED ITS WORST LOSS TODAY
U.S. STEEL 3.1 TO 322.5, BASE METALS .42 TO 70.98 MC1038AES
            (on the long yellow strip)

Now
the pottery is faded and sad
the carmine of the *achiote*
                no longer laughs in the textiles
the textiles became poor
             have lost their style
    fewer threads per inch
        and they do not spin the "perfect thread" any longer
Llacta mama (the soil) belongs to the landowners
the golden butterfly is imprisoned in the Bank
the dictator is rich in money and not in virtues
        and how gloomy
        how gloomy the music of the *yaravies*

The Inca Empire confined forever
        to the unreal kingdoms of the *coca*
            or the *chicha*
    (then only are they free and gay
            and speak loudly
and exist again in the Inca Empire)

In the Puna
            a sad flute
                        a
flute light as a moon ray
            and the moan of a *quena*
with a quechua song . . .
                    Chuapi punchapi tutayaca
                        ("it was night in the middle of the day")
            a shepherd goes by with a herd of llamas
and the little bells jingle
            among the rocks
                            that once were
            a polished wall

Will Manco Capac ever come back with his golden plow?
And will the Indian ever speak again?
Will it be possible
                to reconstruct with these potsherds
                        the gorgeous vase?
To lock again
            in a long wall
                    the monoliths
so that not even a blade fits in the joints?
So that not even a blade fits in the joints
To re-establish the broken causeways
            of South America

toward the Four Horizons
                    with their old couriers?
And will the universe of the Indian become an *Ayllu* again?

The journey was to the Beyond and not to the Museum
            but in the glass case of the Museum
the Mummy still squeezes her pouch of grain
                in her dry hand.

KATUN 11 AHAU

Katun of many arrows and dishonest rulers,
of sadness in the huts,
                                        whispers,
            watchfulness in the night.
In this katun
we weep for the burnt books
and for the exiles from the kingdom. The loss
of the corn
and our teachings of the universe.

Avarice and pestilence and rocks and skulls.

Chief Wild Cat. Chief Honey Bear. The jaguar of the people.
In this katun the chilan writes:
                                "the people eat stones
                        eat twigs."
The katun of the assessment of the tributes,
        of the theft of the mask,
of the theft of the treasure hidden in the milpa.

In this katun there are always invaders,
                    enemies of the land.
O the leeches . . .
                    —They are as gnats to the people.
Emptiers of pots.

And how hard our life in the forest, like badgers.
They have contempt for our knowledge of the book of the universe
for the protection of the people.
          (In this katun they laugh at our costumes).
                The hieroglyphs are lost in the forest.
Our Civilization, under black vultures.
The hurricane rooted out our houses.
The Noblemen are laborers digging on the road.
The people walk hunched with the burden of their mountain in a net.
And the rulers, are like a drought . . .
And we say: if the one
            who built the first arch,
        who composed prayers,
who created the calendar which allowed us to chronicle our history
        and the auguries of the future, were to return.
In the meantime, now, like badgers.
Saddest of moons,
saddest of moons on the sky of Peten.
Oppression . . .
                Watchfulness in the night.
The lewd great Honey Bear . . .

And the chilan writes, "the one who is mouth":
                "Now Great Plagues, great hurricanes are here."
    In the blue sea the fin comes up
    the fin of the
                evil Xooc, Shark, comes up.

But the Katun of the Cruel Men will end.
The Katun of the Tree of Life will be established.
—And a charitable ruler.
No more will they ask the people to ration their food.
The Katun Union-with-a-Cause,
the Katun "Good living conditions."

We shall not whisper any more.
The people will be united, the chilan says.
Many will gather to sing together.
                    Honey Bear will be no more.
The jungle stone will regain its beautiful face.
The square stone
                    will have a face.

There will be good rulers for the happiness of the people.
                    Legitimate lords.
Abundance in the mountains, and beautiful ceremonies.

It is the time to build a new pyramid
                                        over the old pyramid.

The evil Xooc, Shark, will be harpooned.

And there will always be chilans among the people.
Chilan:
                    he who reads the holy scriptures
and studies the sky at night.
—The movements of the Sun and of the Moon
to learn the time for the preparation of the fields,
the harvest of the corn,
                                        the burning of the milpas,
            the setting of the traps,

the search for the deer in the forest.
Chilan: he predicts the days of rain.
The days in which men sing.
The end of the rainy season.
He protects from plague and hunger.
Distributes food in days of hunger.
Supervises the carving of the stelae,
        designs new temples,
turns in the tablets with the eclipses.

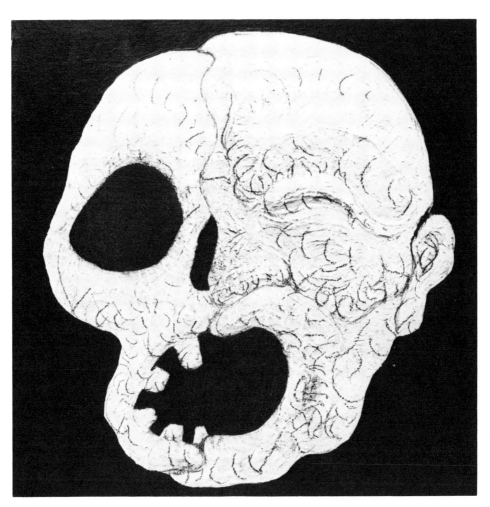

Duality

KAYANERENHKOWA

Sept. Oct.
during these months the migrations take place.
Tanagers from Ohio
        forktail ducks from Oklahoma and Texas
come to Nicaragua.
The cormorant comes from Michigan
                                        to Solentiname
        here they call it *pato-e-chanco.*

        Yes, like airplanes
The New York plane over these lonely places.
            Watching perhaps a color movie
THE PERFECT FURLOUGH
                *** starring Tony Curtis and Janet Leigh***
                        over Solentiname.
And Canadian ducks
                go
in V formation
            Do they come from Lake Ontario?
During these months
        the sky of Nicaragua is full of migrant birds.

And the plover of the Polar Circle
in the wild cove, this *"jungle"**
                              fancy that!
it just flew over Central Park.
                        Or over the United Nations?
Degandawida took his canoe through the lakes . . .

From Niagara Falls to Illinois
                 the *Pax Iroquoia*
"We shall all eat the same beaver from the same plate"
Not only absence of war.
                        The Iroquois peace
was no cold war. They had
the same word for "Peace" and for "Law"
Peace was the right behavior.
Justice in behavior.
The practice of justice among individuals and nations.
Good government was Peace.

                "This it is to be strong, o Chiefs:
                never to be in wrath, not to have quarrels"
Kayanerenhkowa ("the Great Peace")
                —Tarachiwagon, the Great Spirit, inspired it.
The League of Nations was called the "Great Peace"
                and it was sacred.
The priests, the chiefs of the League.
The ax buried so deep so deep
"that nobody should ever see it again in the future"
        But the French gave cannons to the Susquehannock
It was the fur trade . . .

Degandawida the Huron
                who created the New Mentality
(his name means "Master of the Things")
had visions of a new policy.

*In English in the original.

Hiawatha the Onondaga
                    "the one who combs"
(because he combed the snakes out of the minds of men)
was the poet.
He invented the wampum—writing with shells—
and built beautiful stories with shells.
Degandawida took his canoe through the lakes

looking for the smoke on the shore
                              the smoke
of councils.
              Rowing always toward the Dawn.
He crossed Lake Ontario (*Sganydaii-yo*, "the Great Beautiful Lake")
              and no smoke rose.
The Iroquois were at war.
                    The villages
were silent
              surrounded by stockades.
Kayanerenhkowa!!! he shouted

He carried the Mentality of the Master of Life.
        The Good News of Peace
to the camps. Tell the chiefs:
There will be no more wars in the towns
                              the villages will have peace

People should love one another, he said.
A message in the shape of the Meeting House
where there are many fires
                              one for each family
and all together are like one large family
also thus: a union of nations
each nation with the bonfire of its council
and all together will be
                    a great Kanonsionni (Meeting House)

And instead of killing, they will think
                                        Degandawida said.

He arrived at the nation of the Flint (the Mohawks)
and one afternoon he camped by the Mohawk River (New York)
he sat under a tree and smoked his pipe.
            There the League of Nations was founded
            by the Mohawk River (New York)

One afternoon by the lake
Hiawatha the poet was sad
He picked shells on the bank
            and strung them in 3 lines to symbolize his sadness.
And when he lighted his fire, he said:
            "When someone is sad
            as I am now
            I will comfort him with these strings of shells . . ."
(Degandawida came near Hiawatha's smoke)
            ". . . the strings of shells will be words
            and these words that are in my hands
            will be true"
He came near and picked Hiawatha's shells
                        and put them together with others
            and thus
the 2 of them made
                    the laws of the Great Peace
the New Laws with shells
each law expressed by a line of shells
                    the Words of the Great Peace
for the Oneida the Onondaga the Cayuga the Seneca
        the shells of the lake made song
            as the lake sings in the night with its shells
and that song is still sung
in the reservation at night
by the fire.

That was long ago, the Iroquois say
the creation of that UN
       "in the darkness of the past and the abyss of time"
          (1450?)

And the cormorant comes from Michigan . . .
The sun is setting. The jet over La Venada.
Its wake has stayed
          in the sky, long
               looooooooong chalk line
like the Island of La Venada.
   The air-colored lake
   and Cosme's motor boat like floating in the air.
"Look at it sparkle . . ." Don Rafael tells me. Don Rafail.
   Look at it . . .
               Mirror of the Great Spirit!
There they go, there they go, flying in V
           black V V V V V V V
the Canadian ducks
          like flying squadrons
but they change leaders
          and the planes do not change formation.
They probably come from Lake Ontario. They will return
         to Lake Ontario, a new duck
each time at the tip of the V, but always
northward like the needle of a compass
         carrying spring!

Degandawida said
in his first speech of those United Nations:
"The Fire of the Council of the Confederacy of Nations . . . !
But the bonfires of the nations will burn on
and that of each clan

and that of each family
and the bonfire of women and of men
AND THEY WILL NOT BE EXTINGUISHED . . . !"
    And the League of Nations was founded with songs
    delegations in a circle around the fire
           Mohawks and Senecas East of the fire
           Oneidas and Cayugas West of the fire
           Onondagas North of the fire
all singing the same song as a choir.

And at the close of the First Session of the United Nations:
    "My work is done. I
    will enter into the earth. There
    I shall hear how men behave
    in the Meeting House I gave them.
    If the Great Peace ever fails
    if it ever fails
    utter my name in the thicket.
    In the loneliness. And I will return."
They buried axes arrows
    "We have cleaned the earth
        from these things produced by an Evil Mind"
And later the dream of a greater adventure
the meeting around a fire
of *all* the nations of the earth
    the nations of "all the woods on earth"

        A beaver on the plate. Without a knife
        so that nobody should get hurt
        so that no blood is shed

Later, for many years, the hope

that the French would join the League.

>"If you love our souls as you say
>love also our bodies.
>Let us be one nation."

To show their good will
they would deliver themselves unarmed to the French.
With women and children and old men. NOT
as hostages. But

>"to make one nation of the entire earth"

And the march to Quebec—loaded with shells—
but on their way they were attacked by the Algonquins.
The French traded with the Hurons . . .
The talks with the Hurons were blocked.
The agreements with the Hurons, always canceled.
Economic reasons . . . The so-called fur trade . . .
For the Iroquois said: "one nation"
"let us make one people and one nation"
and the French traded with the Hurons.
And the French gave cannon to the Susquehannock.

>*"Let us tame the torrents of the river"*

And they sent 3 canoes of peace to the French.
Those canoes waiting by the fortress.

>"The land will be beautiful, they screamed
>the river will not have waves
>we will live everywhere without fear"

and that evening around the fire with the French
around the symbolic fire:

>"Our faces will melt with yours
>so that we shall also have beards
>and will all become one face"

And the Nation of the Thirteen Fires?
The Nation of the Thirteen Fires did not

>enter the League either.

O
    there went the *ah-weh-ah-ah*.
                It rowed with folded wings.
When the Indians left the Great Lakes
it opened its wings and flew away
and did not come back.

The sound of a radio comes with the wind, from Saba's island.
Saba's radio. Saba (the *cariba,* don Rafail calls her).
Cormorants in line with unfolded wings
            like old shirts on a clothesline.
They wet their tails before flying.
                        Here and in Lake Michigan.
                        Among the buoys of Lake Michigan.
The lakes had a soul, for the Onondaga.
The laws, *talked* in wampum.
                And the treaties in wampum.
            They never broke a wampum
although in treaty after treaty they lost all their land.
The sun sets. Calm lake. In its heart. And an Onondaga moon.
Sept. 25. the first pelicans, 3, by La Venada
flying at water level.
                Tanagers from Ohio. From Kentucky.
                    Like Merton's letter last Tuesday.
And Kennedy Airport so close to Solentiname.
            A radio on an island of a Caribbean Indian.
(Saba brought me oranges)

                We shall all eat the same beaver
                        from the same plate.
Suddenly a fire in the forest, forms spinning
between the fire and the shade, and their shadows spinning
tan-tan   tan-tan   tan-tan, red tattoos

redder now that the flames rise, ah uuuuuuuum
    also children and dogs prancing
                    girls with shells, with
    wampum. Ah uuuuuuuuum. The fire dies off.
They left. And they disappeared from history.
But after the traffic and the neon lights of Syracuse
and beyond the highways in the suburbs, motels
filling stations, and still more neon lights, *HAM & EGGS** at night
behind the large factories, you get to the reservations
a little valley, where that Iroquois said
                  by the old Ford that does not work
      "we will rise again
      and the world will listen to us"

The Good News of Peace for the camps
The Good News of Peace (not AP)
The dead on Roosevelt Avenue. AP was there
        and did not tell.
A man jumped into the middle of the street with arms outspread
          ENOUGH!!!
      and they riddled him with bullets.
Another Somoza will be president.
You told us to call you in the loneliness.
And I am here in Solentiname!
Degandawida! Degandawida!

The murmur as of an outboard motor coming this way
Yet no motor comes this way:
        the airplane
        of the Nation of the 13 Fires . . .
The flight to Panama.
      The friends are not many, and they are far.

*In English in the original.

News from everywhere is bad.
                    If you are as sad as I am now
                    I will comfort you with my wampum,
                                        or with my old Underwood.
With shells. With these typewriter keys.
                                   Not the teletypes.
                    And these words in my hands will be true.
It is the time of the wading birds in Solentiname.
And that of the sad bird that sings *Fucked up*
The last cormorant is gone.
Are the lights on
              at the UN?
DEGANDAWIDA! DEGANDAWIDA!

And where are the jets going?
Are they going
toward Viet Nam?

8 AHAU

Falsities have been heaped on us
Yes, words have attacked us
           The bread of life
     has been cut in half
The talk of the demon *Ah Uuuc,* the seven-deaths
     Now coyotes reign over us
     now alligators are obeyed
Hapai-Can, the Devouring Serpent collects estates
You will say: in that katun there was underdevelopment and so on
               The fierce Ayin, the Alligator
               and the evil Xooc, the Shark.
And over our heads, the vultures of death.
                    In this time of Plebeian Lords . . .
               Falsities. Crazes.
We have been blitzed by evil tongues.
          (Enemies of our food)
Omen of worse governments . . .
We say:
     maybe they will pity the milpas
     Despotism.
               Blood suckers.
     . . . in the meanwhile the Monkey-Lords . . .

Biting she-foxes go from hut to hut
                              collecting taxes
Usurping power
            those conceived in harlots
                  (the sons of bitches)
When power will change hands
when the government of the many comes
                  they will drink from large chocolate mugs
                        they will eat from large communal plates
then the katun will be established
                        the Katun of the Tree of Life
I can see the arrested, imprisoned
                        generals.
            We write in the Book for the years to come.
                  We, the poets
            who protect the people with words.
Prophecies will deceive you
                        if you have contempt for them.
            A Non-Violent katun
Quiet skies over the people's milpas
            . . . in the season of the honey harvest . . .
                  Then they will return the beautiful hut to us.
The road is on painted words
the road we must follow is on painted words.
            Look at the moon, the jungle trees
                  to know when power will change hands.
What kind of stela will we carve?
            My duty is to be the interpreter
                        Your duty (and mine)
            to be reborn.

SQUIRREL OF THE TUNS OF A KATUN

O the eyes of the children cannot read the scriptures.
　　　The books of wood. The writing
　　　　on the stone. And they are as blind . . .
our children.
They cry in the night, Cuy, Horned Owl, Icim, Screech Owl,
　　　　in the ruins.
　　　　　　　　　And when they cry
　　the Indian dies.
The men who sing, scattered.
　　　The jaguars are awarded medals.
　　Military juntas on heaps of skulls
and vultures eating eyes
The dictator-sacrificer-who-tears-human-hearts
　　　　Miss Guatemala murdered
by the *Mano Blanca*
and the United Fruit Co. came to pierce with arrows
the orphan, the widow, the wretched one.
They have eaten Quetzal, they have eaten it fried.
　　　　Haven't they debased us enough yet?
Let us rule to take money from the people, they said
And do they know about our days, about the stars?
　　　the Calendar

like hell they do!
Taxes, to beg from the beggar, from the wretched one.
Chilan Poet Interpreter Priest let it be known
that the first full moon of the katun has already arrived
        pregnant moon
The time in which the President vomits what he swallowed
and the Beauty Queen is reborn in the Police Station
He will say:
                tell me how to go to Chichen Itza
And yes there will be joy for the abundance of the people
                                    (not affliction)
Mayapan will be the place where the katun will change
Cuceb means Revolution
        literally "Squirrel" (that which spins)
It will then be the end of their cupidity and greed.

TAHIRASSAWICHI IN WASHINGTON

In 1898 Tahirassawichi went to Washington
"only to speak about religion"
        (as he told the American government)
     only to preserve the prayers.
And the Capitol did not impress him.
The Library of Congress was all right
but not fit to keep the sacred objects
which could only be kept in his mud hut
        (which was crumbling).
When by the Washington Monument they asked him
if he wanted to go up the elevator or the stairs
he answered: "I will not go up. White men heap
stones to climb on them. I shall not climb up.
    I have climbed the mountains that Tirawa made."
And Tahirassawichi told the State Department:
"Tirawa's hut is the round blue sky
        (we do not like to have clouds between Tirawa and us)
The first thing to do
is to choose a sacred place to live in,
a place devoted to Tirawa, where man
may be silent and meditate.

Our round hut represents the nest
        (a nest to be together in and keep little children)
In the center is the fire which makes us one family.
The door is for anyone to enter
and the visions enter through it.
Blue is the color of Tirawa's hut
and we mix blue dust with river water
for the river stands for life running
through the generations.
The bowl of blue paint is the curve of the sky
and we paint a corncob which is the strength of the earth.
Yet that strength comes from above, from Tirawa
that is why we paint the corncob with the color of Tirawa.
Afterwards we offer tobacco smoke to Tirawa.
        Earlier one did not smoke for pleasure but in prayer
        white men taught the profanation of tobacco to us.
On our way we greet all things with songs
for Tirawa is in all things. We greet the rivers:
from afar the rivers are a line of trees
        and we sing to those trees
closer we see the water line and we hear it
and we sing to the rippling water.
And we sing to the buffalo, but not in the prairies
we sing the *Song of the Buffalo* in the hut
for there are no buffalo left.
And we sing of the mountains, made by Tirawa.
We climb the mountains alone, when we go to pray.
From there we can spot the enemy. Friends as well.
We sing of the mountains for they are good for men.
And we sing of the plateaus, but we sing of them in the hut
for we have not seen plateaus
        those mountains flat on their peaks
but we have been told our fathers saw many plateaus
and we remember what they saw in their journeys.

And we sing of dawn when it breaks in the East
and renews all life
(this is very mysterious, I am telling you
        about something very sacred)
We sing to the morning star
the star is like a man and painted red
      the color of life.
We sing when animals awake
and come out of their lairs where they were asleep.
The doe comes out first, followed by the fawn.
We sing when the sun enters through the door of the hut
and when it reaches the skylight in the center of the hut
and in the evening when there is no more sun in the hut
and it is on the edge of the mountains which are like the wall
of a big round hut where people live.
We sing in the night when dreams come.
For visions visit us easier at nighttime.
They travel better through the sleeping earth.
They approach the hut and stop at the door
and enter the hut, filling it.
If it were not true that dreams came
we would have long forsaken the songs.
And we sing in the night when the Pleiades come out.
The seven stars are always together
and guide the lost, far from their village
(and teach men to be as united as they are).
Tirawa is the father of all our dreams
and extends our tribe through our sons.
With blue water we paint Tirawa's symbol
(an arch with the descending line in the center)
in the face of a child.

        The arch on the forehead and the cheeks
        and the straight line on the nose
(the arch is the blue curve where Tirawa lives

and the straight line his breath that descends and gives us life).
The child's face represents the new generation
and the river water is the passing of the generations
and the blue earth we mix is the sky of Tirawa
(and the blue sketch thus made is Tirawa's face).
Later we ask the child to look at river water
and in the water he sees his own image
as if seeing in his face his children and his children's children
but he is also seeing Tirawa's blue face
portrayed on his face and the future generations.
I told you our hut is like a nest
and if you climb the mountain and look around
you will see the sky surrounds all the earth
and that the earth is round and like a nest
so all tribes may live together and united.
The storm may cast the eagle's nest to the wind
but the oriole's nest only rocks in the wind
        and nothing happens to it."

Tahirassawichi's words, I suppose, did not mean anything
                to the State Department.

Quetzalcoatl

NETZAHUALCOYOTL

The Blossoming Tree is in bloom
in *Tamoanchan*. Tropical flowers
in *Tamoanchan* . . . (As on the chocolate mugs)
Birds suck honey from the Blossoming Tree
and I say: "They surely live here." I hear the blossoming song
as if the mountain were talking
the *zenzontle* sings and the *cascabel-bird* answers
Axayacatl is *zenzontle*, Xicohtencatl *cascabel-bird*
like *teponaztlis*, like drums, like kettle-drums,
gorgeous birds in the flowers. I see
Netzahualcoyotl changed into a quetzal
singing blossoming songs in the Blossoming Tree.
Again as in Texcoco, as in the court, when
they recited in the gardens by a "blossoming-tree."

         They are fishing in the lake;
       the bird sellers come in a boat.
Poets gather in Texcoco.
         The King says: "I am only a minstrel . . ."
The Poet-King, the Philosopher-King (formerly Guerrilla-King)
Changed his name "Strong Lion" to "Hungry Coyote"

(a coyote's head with a knot; the knot means *fasting*)
could it be for his guerrilla years in the mountains?
and he was a Mystic, a Legislator, an Astrologist, an Engineer
                    made poems as well as dams
talking about bridges and new poetry
matters of roads and matters of melody
"these roads are needed"
                              "this dam here"
"and here in Chapultepec we will make a park"
"And which are the new currents?
I mean, the literary currents."
          In the flowery *chinampas* surrounded by philosophers.
He overthrew tyrants and military juntas
                    As for human sacrifices, no. He
                    did not agree.
                              That was not his religion.
Only songs make us great, not war.
                    Surrounded by *tlamatinimes*
                    "the knowers of things"
the words he painted are true.
          Technicians and poets screamed. With
voices of jailed birds, they heard each other
barely.
The coat of arms of Tula, capital of the Toltecs
engraved in stone in the gardens of the Palace.
And after the songs they ate *tacos*
A Poet-Statesman, when there was democracy in Texcoco
                                        strolling
under the avocado trees; he goes with Moctezuma I and other poets
are his buddies
                    "O Moctezuma
               the city of Tenochtitlan will live on
                    only in the paintings of your book"
To be able to tell true words
                    among things that perish.

"For a brief spell, o princes . . ."
Our songs are painted above
here we only blabber, as if asleep.

> The Kings of Texcoco, Tenochtitlan and Tacuba:
> Summit Meeting, to talk about poetry.

All the *tlamatinimes* arrived at Texcoco
and the Emperor was the greatest of the *tlamatinimes.*
this is to Educate: to engrave faces
and he gave faces to others, made sages,
he was a mirror placed before their faces
That the *macehuales* reading the stones, the murals
may find here on earth the meaning of their lives.
The lakes have to be stocked with fish.
A suburb for sculptors
                              and this suburb for painters.
A pyramid for *Tloque Nahuaque*
master of Presence and Privacy
Invisible as night and Impalpable as wind
                    With 9 flights
above, on the outside, only black with stars
                    and no idol inside.
Here across from the pyramid of the Fierce God
and taller than *it.*
Precisely across from the pyramid of Nazi-Huitzilopochtli
the pyramid of the Unknown God, with neither
image nor sacrificial stone in it . . .
Coyote with Knot, Fasting Coyote
prayed alone in there
                    "I am the lone coyote
                    the Hungry Coyote King"
on the terraces, in the tower, lone coyote in the moonlight
hungry for *Tloque Nahuaque*

Tloque Nahuaque who is "Clouded Mirror"
dark, dark as a mirror of obsidian
                    hard to see as lake in the fog
                 obsidian lake in the moonlight
The *teponaztli* plays all night in Tlaloc's temple.
The *huitzilopochtlist* sons of bitches.
              the sacrificed roll down the steps
Flute of the Clouded Mirror
coyote howling in the moonlight
alone, far from the herd
Netzahualcoyotl sings on the terrace
              "I did not know it before, and was sad . . .
              I did not have happiness in anahuac.
              I anxiously longed for
                       the flowers of things!
              I did not know it very well, and was sad.
              Is it possible that some may never know it?"

They sang their wars in sheds in Colhuacan
("for he was seen in pain, whipped by the wind")
sheds of romantic Atotoztli and of Coxcotzin from Chalco
                  ("To the site of the danger he goes
                  to the site of the danger he goes")
they sang in Colhuacan
and at 40 and unmarried
Hungry Coyote with no girl at night
without a girl of sweet rubber neck
in the night.
Only songs
        for sadness
Even a little beauty frees from sadness
and sadness scatters with the kettle-drums
                like mist on Lake Texcoco
                there toward Tenochtitlan

you play the *chichitl*
            which when you pluck it says "chich, chich . . ."
you play, play, your timbrel and you sing
Lone Heart, Hungry Heart, you sing:
            Bring your inspiration
            to our poor clay timbrel, to our
            poor stone drums, wood drums
            the sound of the clay flute are your flowers o God
He made his books
in the Black Mansion, place of meditation and fasting
            The Black Mansion is his house of paintings.
"Military men destroy our books"
The Poet Lone Coyote asked for a light.
Even a small light the size of a firefly
to look for the true God.

The Kings arrived at Texcoco requesting advice
And all the poets arrived at Texcoco
modern painters for the murals, to
paint flowers, animals on the new walls
and on the maguey paper and the deer skin
Musicians, sculptors, goldsmiths, ceramists.
The Scientists. The Intellectuals.
            Poets of the *chinampas* of Xochimilco
            of Tenochtitlan where they are burning books
Architects from Azcapotzalco, from Tenochtitlan
Surveyors to measure the land of the people
conscientious draftsmen to paint it on the books
yellow flower-that-paints all of the people
clearly marked, clearly designed boundaries.
And they took into the palace
the red, green, white, sky-blue soils
carmine-colored soil, brown colors
colors to paint skies, faces, flowers.

And the tributes on *amate* paper arrived.
Janitors let the color vendors in
bringing grass-green, *achiote*-red, chile-red
for the books, not to daub colonels.
Feathers for mosaics, not for uniforms
of Eagles and Tigers. Exotic animals for the zoos
brought from the land of the rubber trees.
The one goes after butterflies; another after melodies
the one watches flowers and yet another, constellations.
Historians reconstruct the pilgrimages with colors
and the long line of kings standing in the Region of Mystery.
And the King goes from room to room wearing blue-jeans
inspecting the work. "This engraving is imperfect"
Or he says: "see if the widows are well"
"Study the stars too"
They are painting the BORGIA CODEX
                    "There is a rain of flowers in Texcoco"
Acolhuacan was full of songs

                                tracks show a road . . .
                    2 spayed magueys giving water-honey . . .
                                2 vessels with pulque . . .
                        some hallucinogenic mushrooms . . .
                Quetzalcoatl plucking a strange instrument . . .
The setting: a banquet with songs the gods make
            "There is a rain of flowers in Texcoco"
Now you paint a picture of singing poets
"I, the Poet Hungry Coyote, say it:
            as an *elote* flower opening briefly
            thus we have come to dream in Meso-America . . ."
They gather in the Poetry Room.
The Giver of Life paints things with Beauty
colors with Flower-Song
                        things are his Codex
those colors of the lake, ruby silver of flowers
are his *flowers and songs,* his poems
                        we live only in his painting

We come near him with poems, with paintings.
We make songs in honor of the One who invents himself
     and is the inventor of things
and he is in the songs
     not in the "blossoming wars" but in FLOWER-SONG
 and gives the poems
while we smoke.
    "We shall be in Texcoco for a short time
    my friends
a short time here in Texcoco.
My house is there, where one lives with no body.
We all leave, we all leave, brother"
    And Cuacuauhtzin sings:
      "Let us all be friends!
      let us know each other through songs.
      We are leaving but the songs will remain.
      I hear a song and I become sad . . .
      The rains arrived and yet I cry.
      I shall leave rain, flowers and songs behind.
      That is why I cry, that is why I sing."
"You are friends of the Brotherhood, of the Society."
    Lake Texcoco full of canoes.
    Canoes and *chinampas,* with girls.
    Smoke of human sacrifices
    far way over Tenochtitlan.
     And white against the sky, the Sleeping Woman.
"The Society, the Brotherhood of poets
    will not disappear because of me"
And Axayacatl, the young poet sings:
      "If I were to be killed tomorrow . . ."
And Cahualtzin sings after him and Xicohtencatl after him.
Netzahualpilli, the child poet, romps in the "blossoming tree"
Xochiquetzal, the Minister of Poetry is over there.
    The flowers are perfect
    in Tamoanchan . . .

Tochihuitzin the pacifist is there
Tochihuitzin from Tenochtitlan, the anti-huitzilopochtlist.
Tlaltecacatzin prince-poet, asks for political advice.
                Lake Texcoco, sky colored
                jade colored by the shore;
                a heron flies towards Huexotla
                    with the color of the "pop-corn" flower.
They neither drank *pulque* nor ate mushrooms.
                        They were not bohemians.
            They pass the religious pipe around
                and gain inspiration with the mugs of cacao.
        Xochiquetzal was slow in combat
        but quick to capture beauty.
Ayocuan, the mystical poet, the *teohua*
"owner of the things of the gods," says:
                "Did you too talk to God?
Have you spoken to the God?
Earth is the region of the fleeting moment.
Our father God comes down
to the kettle-drums, the tambourines, the tortoise shells.
The Only God is worshipped thus."
Tecayehuatzin, prince of Huexotzinco, says:
                "Ayocuan Cuetzpalzin
has certainly come near God."
Tochihuitzin says:
                    "you knit flowers
                and I only knit hay"
And Ayocuan, the *teohua*-poet sings:
"My house of the paintings is your house too, Only God"
There the king awards the prizes for the poems
        a golden nose-pendant for the poet Chichicuepon
      for Tozmauetzin blankets of duck down . . .

At night Netzahualcoyotl was alone in his palace
From the terrace he looks at the stars

at the Truncated Pyramid of the cosmos with its Nine Flights
yearning to climb it.
Invisible as night and impalpable as wind.
A difficult friend . . .
In this way we will perhaps stop being beggars (with the songs)
                        How can anyone reign on the earth?
It hides from us . . .
                            Will our friends
                        live again?
We are perhaps like a broken mosaic
                        that will gather anew.
I, Emperor Netzahualcoyotl, have not come to reign here.
"Does he exist?" "Or does he not?"
            He, the Night and Wind, does not answer this question
I am searching for someone among the flowers.
I wish
we will be alive there, be alive, yes
where there is no Calendar nor counting of days nor book
                                    of the years
can on ayac micohua
            "where death does not exist"
can on ayac micohua
            finally my heart has understood!
There, that I may go
that I may go where there is no death
where death has been sacrificed and thrown down the steps.
                    Fragrant flowers, fragrant flowers
                    my wisdom was vain.
And Azcalxochitzin was so pretty.
                Her smell of "pop-corn" flower.
With her Aztec style make-up and her feathery mini-skirt
she looked like a little bird of the land of rubber.
                                    Miserere mei
        I want *flowers* that will last in my hands.
I am searching for someone among the flowers.

                    In the afternoon he is painting his poems.
He looks from the Library
                    at coves color of quetzal
the *yapalli*-green islands against the *tejotli*-blue lake
the sky as painted with blue grass
and on the edge of the water, heron-colored Texcoco
the temples painted *tizatl*-white
                    We live only in your paintings, Giver of Life.
And as figures erased on a codex
the Society of the Poets will be erased from your paintings.
                    Like a careful painter that paints and erases.
You cross us out with your black-*tlilli* ink of torch-smoke
your ink like night and the hair of Azcalxochitzin.
Tlaloc's drums play all night.
                    They climb the pyramid in line
                    breathless, snorting, they are too fat.
                    Those *tamales* will not have any *chile*.
"To humanize the affection of the people"
            "To give them faces" (moral features)
With *nocheztli*-red and herb-green and lake-blue
you paint your words Netzahualcoyotl
and your heart is in the codex.
The Giver of Life
lives in you, writes in you.
                    They are hunting ducks on the shore.
            The canoes go from Texcoco to Tenochtitlan.
You drive us out of our minds, Giver of Life
as with a meal of hallucinogenic mushrooms
        (one feels glued to the wall and does not speak any more
        another sees himself climbing the pyramid and sobs
        another sees that he will be rich and buy people
        and when the effect is over they tell each other what they have seen)
You intoxicate us like *pulque*, and like the *pulque* of war
        the intoxication of death, and the end of man
        and now, drunk again, they go stumbling to the pyre.

FLOWER-SONG (poetry): May it not wilt!
Flower-Song is dialog and Duality comes.
Flowers and Songs, word of the Night and Wind.
May it not wilt. May it not wilt.

In Tenochtitlan, Itzcoatl, puppet of Tlacaelel
is burning books.
He and Tlacaelel. They say
            "it is better that the people not know the paintings"
(those that are held)
                    "will spoil
        and the earth's course will be swayed"
Jades? I, Netzahualcoyotl, am an expert in fine jades
fluted jades, "quetzal" jades, and so on. . .
and I tell you: friendship is the best jade.
                        "I remember it all
                                and am sad"
May the songs be lasting, the metaphors
                    as the skull of rock crystal
                    as the diorite mask
        Thus only can one live on earth . . .
Few become real on earth
with poems
            in *anahuac* (the earth) they become real.
I think that future generations
        will be more worthy of knowing him . . .
Dawn. The big star flees
The *zacuan* bird sings
The fog is over Tenochtitlan
And a girl far from his life, farther
                    than the Sleeping Woman.
In this season the ducks leave, where do the ducks go
when they leave?
even if you are made of jade . . .
                        even if of gold . . .

"Perhaps the Empire of Azcapotzalco will not last long!"
                    the people would say
And Azcapotzalco fell. He himself killed the dictator.
Now historians paint his history.
The triumphs, and the sadness too . . .
The murder of king Ixtilxochitl his father.
His childhood in a rural hamlet in the mountains. First love.
Here from the pyramid they announce his death sentence.
            Here he burns the temple of Azcapotzalco.
Here a little king sits and on his head
                    sits an even smaller woman (a dream)
        Azcalxochitzin!

"The King has riches yet he is poor"
                    he told the logger and his wife.
In the construction of the "Netzahualcoyotl" dam
the Emperor himself carried logs, carried rocks.
And afterwards he built the zoo at Chapultepec.
More magueys have to be planted in my kingdom
                    Look after those widows
Fruit trees for the kids
it is well known that boys like fruits
More songs and dances for the *macehuales*
One day he said:
            "Buy everything there is in the market
Don't haggle and distribute it freely.
Hurry, before I eat."
                    I am a *macehual*, Netzahualcoyotl said
He would go to the markets in disguise
to listen to complaints against the government, to know
what the people thought.
            In disguise, as in the time of the guerrillas
He wrote 80 laws
            he who moves milestones must die

each law meditated with prayer and fasting
                he who commits adultery must die
And if the son-in-law of the King commits adultery
he must die.
He established strict forestry regulations
for the conservation of the forests
but he saw a child gathering sticks at the edge of the wood
and softened the law.
He forgave a criminal because of some verses he wrote.
He ordered the doors of the palace to open
to the poor, to the market people, to the *macehuales.*
                He disliked the smell of the priests
          dressed with the skin of flayed men.
"Let's plant corn, *ayote,* beans
at the edge of the roads
                for travelers, for the poor,
it will not be theft, they will not die for it."
         No trial will last over 80 days
with all its petitions and appeals
Do not allow the taxes to increase
Nor the *tamales* to change in size
         Do not allow the rich to oppress the *macehuales.*
Universal education should be compulsory
             The 2 subjects of university teaching:
    Ixtlamachiliztli ("to give wisdom to the faces")
      Yolmelahualiztli ("to straighten the hearts")
death penalty for historians
who (knowingly) falsify the truth of the facts in their paintings.
Judges worked morning and afternoon
                    (except on holidays)
had lunch in the palace. The Ministry of Poetry
was open all day long. The Ministry of War
was generally closed.
Intelligent and honest, that is how bureaucrats should be
Otherwise laws are worthless

It was mandatory for public officials
                    to listen to songs. Bribes
were penalized with death.
Poets and artists exempt from taxes
(Beauty is their tax)
                    Composers of bad music were fined.
And thus Texcoco was the city of beauty
Around Lake Texcoco every city in peace
Few prisoners for the gods. "The sun is thirsty"
priests complained.
                    Clichés
Tlacaelel's slogan
of the nazi-Aztecs.
          Our offerings of human hearts
              our sacrifices to the Sun
                                are the songs
No individual dictatorship, no one party.
                    His great shadow was the *pochote* tree
              "Caudillo prince of poets"
Presiding the Brotherhood of the Singers
          . . . in the afternoons when the brotherhood gathered . . .
          Kettle-drums in the breeze on the quiet lake
let terror, tyranny
perish on earth with joy.
Flute of God
              "a wise face"
He shone in Texcoco like a smokeless torch
Of no king were so many things painted
He was more famous for his verses than for the 44 kingdoms
And he found emptiness everywhere

                    Tlacaelel raised to astronomical figures
                    the number of human sacrifices
                    Huitzilopochtlist Tlacaelel.
My ideology is Non-Violence, Netzahualcoyotl said.

There was hunger in the year of 10-Rabbit
(snow on a house, on people and on trees)
                    and Netzahualcoyotl opened the barns.
          Distributed corn to the people
6-Rabbit (*chapulin* eating a plant)
               gave corn tortillas, for the weak
2-Cane (a vulture is seen on a corpse)
          "Give us water" they told him
          And the King said: "There is plenty in the mountains"
and brought it with acqueducts from Yelloxochitlan.
The world did not end and they lit a new fire.
Others
led the people first through shortcuts of rabbits and deer
Tezozomoc, Maxtla . . . Those who had hearts like cacti
Now the artists, the poets: "a heart with god"
               the creators of realities
the discoverers of the Flower-Song
                    the only way
               of telling truth on earth
The owners of precise language and careful expression
Who give a language to the *macehuales.* The masters
of the science of *tecpillatolli* ("exact language")
Poetry is for the *macehual*, Netzahualcoyotl used to say
A *true language* like the nahuatl of Quetzalcoatl
The tradition of the Toltecs blossomed there in Texcoco
"followers of the old doctrine" (of Quetzalcoatl)
The Toltecs, the wise people, the "singers"
who founded the old cities with a song
                    "because it is said
                       that the cities started thus
                       music was in them"
and they died but left a stone forever
quivering
their hopes, their shivers were left to us in a paper, in a kettle-drum,
and their voice speaks in the old men, in the knowers of books

in the sages chaste as children and already blind
with hair as fiber of maguey.
They are still teaching how to be a Toltec
                              in the "houses of song"
Schools of Arts patronized by Quetzalcoatl
            the painters are *Toltecs* of the ink
                  the poets are *Toltecs* of the word
and the King-Poet Netzahualcoyotl: the great Toltec.

When he died there was no mourning.
                              There were festivities in Texcoco
Music in the palace, folk dances on the streets
as by his wishes.
In the villages they said: "Has he died?"
"Or hasn't he died?"
"Would he have gone on a long trip
                  like maybe to Tehuantepec?"
"Or is he gone as Quetzalcoatl who left without dying
and will return?"
            O Netzahualcoyotl
you have already gone to the region of mystery
Will he return?
I, singer, cry when remembering Netzahualcoyotl
        O Netzahualcoyotl
nobody lives twice
Will Netzahualcoyotl and Netzahualpilli
            chat there, at the place of the Kettle-drums?
        I wish Ayocuan White Coyote could make you
        happy if only for a minute!
The meeting is held there.
He asks:
            "How is the land of Acolhuacan now?"

"Yes
they live here, there is no doubt." He is that quetzal.
By the river of jade and under the Blossoming Tree
the musical birds sing for the Inventor of Life
They took me to the heart of the Blossoming Land
to the mountains of the Land-of-our-food
There I finally saw the flowers and the songs.
            "tell me, how is the land of Acolhuacan now?"
Come once again to the lake to preside
at the meeting of President-poets among flowers and songs.
Put on your head your crown of flowers
o king Netzahualcoyotl

CAUSEWAY

We are opening a causeway
to Chichen Itza
                    all of us from the town
to connect our village of Chan Kom
with Chichen Itza.
Even though tourists will never come
and the causeway will not yield profits.
("The Causeway of Light"
                    all of us from the town call it.)
Many miles are still to be done
but from the tallest trees
in the jungle, we see far away
on the horizon
                a little white triangle:
          the ruins of the Castle
                of Chichen Itza.

MILPA

The corn is buried, invisible as the dead
in your milpa
       Only many little mounds of soil
like the pyramids of the dead
             in the milpa of the dead.
Yet the *chac* with their gourds will come
      (their *machetes* are strokes of lightning)
     the drippers
the transparent, rain-colored *chac*
     sink in the *cenotes*
and gather in the nights of June in the ruins at Coba.
And the *balam* will come, the guardians of the milpas
     with their air-colored bodies
the *balam* who fly invisibly over the trees, and you can
hear them whistle, you can hear them
whistle at night in the roads herding the evil spirits.
And the *x-kol* bird will sing in the milpas
    to make the corn grow
        grow more grow more
             (from plant to plant)
   and to make the corn happy.

With the eastern wind the rains will come
they will come from the East, from where the sun rises
     and the moon and the stars rise
from the East, where the ruins of Coba are.
And there are the animals of the dreams
       about which the hunters talk
animals with long hair, spotted or striped animals like tigers
strange animals that have only been seen in dreams
and that haunt the ruins of Coba.
In the soil the grains, step by step
     one step a day
are climbing the pyramid of corn.
The night is full of very shiny stars
sign of rain.

PAWNEE MARCHES

A blanket. Colored beads
a pipe carved by Blue Hawk
                    freely from tribe to tribe
not in a commercial but in a religious exchange
freely, throughout the wide expanses
of the USA.

        Those were the prairies crossed by the Pawnees.

Where the plants of the Boeing Corp. are
                    necrophilic
or of Dow the makers of napalm
                            necrophilic
the Dow Corp. (condoms and napalm)
                    life hater
            "it was in the Spring, when the birds mate
            or in the Summer, when they make their nests"
and the highways where the green convoys ride
laden with weapons

those were the prairies crossed by the Pawnees
              "or in the Fall, when they fly in flocks.
              Not in the Winter, when life is asleep"
              General Motors 11.7%
              American Motors 7%
       $870.8 billion, an increase of 8%
              commercial ads in the sky
written by planes
              and the roar of the RS-71 and of the A-11 in the sky
              sinister wings
                 bullet shaped body

the Pawnees, in the procession of peace.
Under the skies of Kansas.

And, *man!**
the Chamber of Commerce VP
of Wichita, Kansas says
     this economy is booming. The fact is,
   if the war stops tomorrow
you're going to have some panic

The spirits of men and animals
could leave their bodies and travel far away.
Thus also the spirits of people
              could gather . . .

Johnson said "peace epidemic" (*Time*, Feb. 17, 1967)

Those songs were dreamt, they say
those rites and those songs were dreamt
in earlier times by their ancestors

                          The winds are invisible
                          yet they are very strong

*In English in the original.

Once a priest traveled over a prairie
and he saw a nest hidden in the grass and he said to himself
if my people were to learn from the birds
my tribe would be happy, full of children.

       (A bombing halt
           Rusk says
   "is practically an obscene proposal")

Over those prairies
over prairies and mountains.   And it was impressive.
Sometimes for a few miles; others, for 100 miles or more
(Tahirassawichi had taken the procession as far as the Omahas)
Something very different to those groups of hunters
or warriors, or mere travelers.
     And not only to ask for abundance:
but above all to establish unity
between two groups, a kind of communion
       "and so that there may be peace among the tribes"
It had to be between two peoples, two clans or two tribes
necessarily two different communities
    (and sometimes they were antagonistic).
One group marched toward the other with songs
the chiefs ahead with their eagle feathers
advancing silently, rigidly, staring ahead
the singers with the wooden drums behind them
     and lastly the horses with the gifts.
It was also barter of goods
and thus arts and crafts of one tribe
traveled freely from tribe to tribe
across the USA.
     In the endless prairie, for miles and miles
  holding their formation
       day after day.

And if a group of warriors sighted them from the peak of a mountain
they did not attack, knowing they carried symbols
stronger than weapons.
                    They returned to their villages in peace.

Can there be peace
without bankruptcy?
                    Electra produces 100 million a year
for Lockheed (Electra = patrol plane)
And what profits do the Polaris missiles
                    and the F-104 produce
                    for Lockheed?

                                        The winds are invisible
                                            yet they are very strong
All water is holy.
The white men taught the Indians the profanation of the tobacco plant.
Winds sun earth plants water
are Minor Powers between Tirawa and man.
          —You must not picture Tirawa as a man.
A priest heard a bird singing one morning
with shriller and happier notes than the others
he looked for it and found it was the sparrow, the weakest one
and he told himself: this is a lesson for my people
every one can be happy and have a song.

I have done what has never been done
said the *kúrajus* to Miss Fletcher
          I have given you the songs
perhaps my life was kept for this
                    to sing the sacred songs
in the great flute.

What are you going to do with the production?*
                (the VP points to Boeing)
"What are you going to do with the production
and what about jobs for those 400,000 people over there"
                    (pointing to the prairies owned by Boeing)
"if peace came?"

The voice of the old *kúrajus* in the old gramophone
What the wise Pawnee *kúrajus*
left behind (sang) in the great flute.
        The great flute: Miss Fletcher's gramophone.

*In English in the original.

ORACLES OF TIKAL

(from an AH KIN of KU)

What the sacred paintings and the signs say
        that the Ah Kins, Priests-of-the-Solar-Cult
saw in the upright stones, the stelae of the katuns
the prophecies of the great sages, the great Ah Kins:
           the end of greed and plunder
        the katun of the communal food
when the katun changes, when the establishment changes
           Power and Bank will loose their might
                    their arrows will rot
the Jaguars will be stripped of their spots
        of their claws
the Oligarchy of the Batabes Those-of-the-Ax the climbers
        will be lost
              their Gourd will be taken away
Ku, Deity, is now weeping
        we have drunk terror as if it were porridge
all have fallen with their burden
    And for so many tuns
        so many tuns
              the Books are not read.
  The cenote-wells will dry up at this time

It is night in the Peten
                the place of the huge tilted carved stones
Ah Maax Cal, the Blabber-Monkey talks and talks
                . . . and a delicate sadness in the eyes of the Indians
with no electricity in their night
                        Electricity in the nuts
        cast away like deer
the shadow of the barracks at Mayapan is long
Colonels, Generals:
        we are fed up with their lewd semen
The hooded torturers
                Doris' rapists.
        On our faces they placed the weeping mask
            our gourd laden with bitterness
        . . . their empire of despotism
                        Generation of Apes
intervention
                        They have castrated the sun.
The President with sacrificial flint
Mayapan of Deer Victims
Woe, the Major comes with electrical connections
And Monsignor has seen no wounds
has seen nothing
Our texts are only in the trees, in the animals
                (that is why they scorn them)

The speeches of Ah Maax Cal, the Blabber-Monkey
                Great Rottenness
and saddened skies
Ubico, Carias, the Somozas
            How much are we to give to sate them?
Ubico put us to work for free on the highways.
        The hieroglyph lost
                    and its teachings lost with it

The Oligarchy of the Batabes, Those-of-the-Ax, hail of the earth
        Those-of-the-Ax.
           Formerly we walked upright
The foreign exploiters, those
        with party clothes
      blood suckers
                  men-animals
the great blood sucking adulterous general
words that I, Chilam Balam, say weeping
      I, Ku's interpreter
His orgies and his chaos will be shown
but when they are over:
      what the young will see
in the hieroglyphs of day and night will be different.
As you see that star over your hut in the evening
so will the revolution shed light on your life.
The people will leave their dense jungles, their quarries
      This is what he who fasts sees
. . . when misery is relieved
      my words will be remembered
That which was learned in the nights of Tikal, Place-of-Seclusion
It will be the time of dawn and of wakefulness
    the change of the plates, the change of government
and from the dense jungles and from the quarries
    they will bring their teachings
this may happen
      this may not happen
The people will take over the Government, the Bank
    (another word will come)
we will tear the hoofs, the fangs of the Incumbent
  you will no more turn your maidens over to the Gambling Casino
foreigners will no longer call us "The Land of the Deer"
    Land-of-very-good-deer
poor orphaned fawn licking all hands!
When the opossums devour one another

the time when the red Jaguars tear one another apart
                    one another apart
The people will sit down to eat
              They will snatch their gourds, their plates
another word, other teachings will come
arising from deep wells, from caves
          They will again clothe their bodies in white.
          The Sterile Lords will remain behind
that is stated in the paintings on the walls
    it will then be dawn
the fall of Ah Chac Chibal, the Great-Meat-Eater
the land will no longer open its legs to the gangsters
              to the invaders
Such will be the true end of the blood suckers
              Along the sea coast we will mock
the evil Xooc, Shark
          the Uo frogs will croak at noon in their puddles
new wisdom will come, new words
              and the face of Ku, Deity, will be manifest
when the change of power comes
and the Ah Kins will also change, Priests-of-the-Solar-Cult
maidens will sing in the cenote-wells in the moonlit nights
calling their long gone lovers, and the lovers will return
and the Ah Kins will be able to talk to one another
          Priests-of-the-Solar-Cult
and the Chilanes will be heard
                          with their ocarinas
    music will return
the jingles will sound in the sky of the Peten
      it may happen, it may not

      —"He who keeps the Book in his bosom."
I come from afar, from Tikal, Place-of-Seclusion
      The carved stones which are in the heart of the Peten.

The Quetzal will open its wings in the sky of Guatemala
Yaax Imiche, Green-Ceiba-Tree, will bloom again
thus
the Ah Kin Chilam Balam read in the wheel of the katuns
this is what he interpreted from the signs painted in the book
following the explanation of the painted signs
as they appear in the signs in the books
      thus spoke the interpreter of the sacred writings
      prophet of the deep wells, of the caves.
This will be understood when there lives an Ah Kin with
    whole and saintly soul.

Four Creator Gods and Crucifixion

THE GHOST DANCE

"These lands are ours
nobody has the right to take them away
we were their first owners"
Shooting Star to Wells, 1807
And the President could rest in peace in his great Village
drinking his wine in peace
while he and Harrison would have to fight
Shooting Star to Harrison, 1810
The Great Spirit gave this great island to his sons
the Red Skins . . .
They have pushed us from the sea to the Great Lakes
we can go no farther!
Tecumseh (or "Shooting Star") would say
—He had hoped the whites would stop at the Ohio . . .
And that magnificent Confederacy of
poor
ragged, hippy tribes
from the Great Lakes to Mexico
. . . "with no intention of declaring war on the United States!" . . .
dreamt by Tecumseh, the meteor, Shooting Star!
(He would build an Empire like Moctezuma's or
the Incas', Harrison informs the State Department

"if it were not for the vicinity of the United States")
They returned every year in the Spring:
they came up, from the South northward, with Spring
and their arrival was as predictable as Spring
When the first touches of green
                   were seen, the
first flowers (tracks
of God's moccasin on the prairies)
there on the horizon . . . a dot . . . several dots . . .
             many dots!!!
        and the prairie was a huge mass of buffalo.

The Great Spirit gave us this land
so that we might light our fires here.
                                        Here
we will stay. And as for borders
the Great Spirit does not acknowledge borders
and his sons, the Red Skins, will not acknowledge them either . . . .
                              (Shooting Star)
Afterward Kanakuk, a new prophet:
             if a white man strikes, do not complain.
It is bad to have witchcraft and charms.

—Herds of twenty of two hundred of ten thousand of
              ten million buffalo
twenty miles fifty miles two hundred miles
         wide (the length was unknown)
         the entire earth throbbing with buffalo
and the lowing was heard from 2 miles from 3 miles
away—

("if it were not for the vicinity of the United States")

. . . The Great Spirit placed us on this land
                    why do you wish to take it away from us?

General Clark, my Father
                I speak and speak
so that you may have pity on us
and allow us to remain where we are.
Clark, my Father, when I finish speaking,
I want you to write to the President the Great Father
that we wish to remain here a little longer
and now I will speak to the President the Great Father
President Great Father I want you to think about us
I wish to speak with peaceful and tender words
some chiefs said that the land belongs to us Kickapoos
that is not what the Great Spirit told me
the land belongs to Him
when I saw the Great Spirit he told me: say it to the President
he told me to throw away our tomahawks
Since I talked to the Great Spirit
my people do not have food they are poorly dressed
He did not tell me to sell my land
because I do not know the value of a dollar
you know how to write how to copy what is said
not I who do everything by the Great Spirit
all things belong to the Great Spirit
I am already done I trust in the Great Spirit

Summers they spent in Montana
they were in Nebraska and Wyoming in the Winter
                    snowed prairies black with buffalo
          and the Indians would go North with the buffalo
and in the Winter southward to Texas
with the buffalo.

Night of the prairies, big fires
                    far away
      as now by night in Denver
as when one approaches Denver by night in a Greyhound bus

But they were fewer each year
the herds were fewer each year.
YOU MUST NOT FIGHT was the teaching of Wowoka
                    they stopped drinking whisky
            they removed the scalps from their tents.
The doctrine of the Paiute was dance.
The buffalo that migrated to the South at the beginning of Winter
                running against the wind
            and moved from South to North in the spring
                        running against the wind
were fewer each year.
            Tuhulhulsote by the fire: we
have never traded
the land is part of my own body
I never sold my land.

                    The buffalo left the prairies
                    and the Indians left with the buffalo.

To dance to dance
                everywhere. All the Indians must dance.
Very soon, next Spring
the Great Spirit will come
with all the game again
and all the dead Indians again
Go on dancing go on danc-
ing in the prairies.
                    Better times will come.
ALL THE DEAD WILL BE BORN AGAIN Wowoka said
                Jack Wilson (Wowoka)
war is bad and they shouldn't fight
the entire earth later will be good
            brothers, they will all be brothers
Indians and Whites forming one people.

A fire. The new faith ran like a fire
blown by the wind of the prairies.
      The red paint was sunrise
          eagle feathers the rays of the sun
            the eagle was the sun
he who carries the feathers is at one with God
he carries the "Presence" in his head
        The Eagle will come to take me
        The Eagle will come to take me

Smohalla in his tent on the banks of the Columbia river
        smoking his sacred cigarette
          "we are few and weak
            we cannot resist."
The word coming from Washington, D.C. was bad
        In the beginning all was water and God was alone
he felt very lonely and created the earth.
        Man had wings and flew wherever he wanted
but man felt lonely and God made a woman.
God sent man to hunt
        and the woman to cook and to prepare the furs.
The great river was full of salmon and the prairies full of buffalo
The strongest chose the best fishing waters
God became angry and took their wings away
ordered that the fishing waters and the fields belong to all
that there should be no more borders nor divisions
        this is the old law. They
who divide the land and sign papers
      will be punished by God.
The word that comes from Washington, D.C. is bad.
All the dead will live again
      We shall not leave, for
the people must wait *here,* on this land, for their return.

And, in dreams,
                    their wisdom.
     It was learned in dreams
                         Smohalla would say.
"The boys of my tribe will not work
          men who work do not dream.
     We shall never be rich like the whites."

And an Umatilla chief (clouds of dust of the last buffalo
far away, cacti, western movie setting
and the tent of buffalo hide shaken by the wind)
          :you tell me, go to another land
               I want no money for my land.
. . . and the wind brings from the camp
the melody of
     a protest song.

The buffalo was the Universe
               the totality of manifested forms
and food dress housing artifacts and so on it was all made
                              from the buffalo.

In 1810 there are no more buffalo in Kentucky
          The next day (January 1)
               there were no more buffalo in Pennsylvania
                    Xmas 1802 the
                         last buffalo in Ohio was killed
And nothing, they did not avoid the arrival of white men,
every year more whites
          the railroads brought more whites
               the buffalo were disappearing from the prairies
and the railroad moving forward, forward

                    the rails cutting the fields of the Indians
            and they lost the freedom of the prairies
carried each time farther, to
more distant reservations
            they disappeared like the buffalo of the prairies
            and their traditions and their songs vanished
            with the buffalo.
Your spring flower-eating buffalo!
Vachel Lindsay!
used to run where now locomotives run.
        Your Spring flower-eating buffalo!
And the gold rush. The gold
attracted more whites.
                        The last buffalo to be seen in Montana
                        tired, limping, almost unable to run
                        surrounded by wolves
An old Arapaho very old in his old tent
            rotten buffalo hide
    :"the grass is old
    our life, old
    this land very old.
            Everything will be new again."

And the Indians in the Southern prairies said
            "rivers mountains
            everything looks old and will be renewed"
The dance passed from tribe to tribe
            (ember of a dead fire
                which was fanned, fanned
                by the wide wind of the prairie
        revives and burns prairies and prairies)
THE GHOST DANCE was without weapons

night after night dancing the sacred dance
        There were tribes that left their firearms
          and even everything made of metal
      "everything as it was before the whites"
In Oklahoma it was said the new land would come from the West.
              With all the dead Indians
all the dead since the beginning of time, reborn
        with reborn buffalo, bison, deer.
And some returned to their tribes with the tale: Jesus
came back to earth. The whites killed him
beyond the Great Waters, now
he has come where the Indians are, who never harmed him.
The days of the past will return. The
buffalo will also return.
           It is evil to shoot others.
The Great Spirit does not want it.
And in Nevada, another prophet, a Paiute:
Above all, no more wars
        Love one another
let us all dance
            MAKE LOVE NOT WAR *
   To be at peace with the whites
And the Sioux said
(the buffalo-less Sioux):
              They are coming
all the dead tribes are coming
        and with them are the great herds of buffalo
alive again
        coming from the prairies of the Great Spirit.
   All the animals will soon be returned to the
Indians
      next Spring
  when the grass reaches the knee
        on the day of the general resurrection.

*In English in the original.

With no weapons in their hands
                but with hands in hands
                          dancing in a circle
(red was dawn)
            Thus said the Father
            let us all sing on earth
            let them carry his message far
            let them carry his message far
(The feathers on their heads were wings
              to fly to the
                      prairies of the sky)
In 1889 the Oglala overheard
that the son of God had come to the West
        and the Oglala danced.

Hand in hand.
            The dance passed from tribe to tribe.
Pacifism, sit-ins, non-violence.
    "We want to live with the whites like brothers"
They saw in the trances of the Dance the world of the spirits
        all the tents of new buffalo hide
the riding spirits returning from buffalo hunts
in the moonlight, loaded with buffalo meat
      and the prairies with thousands and thousands of buffalo.
The Ghost Dance was without weapons
And some who had been to the nation of the Indian spirits
said:
           "The nation of the dead Indians is returning
        returning
      and THE GREAT SPIRIT is returning to his Red Indians."
AND
. . . "in the land of the men-spirits
    I saw a teepee
    and at the door of the teepee a man-spirit

told me: the white men and the Indians must dance
together; but first they should sing.
There should be no more wars."

They saw the spirits camping on the prairies of the sky
driving the stakes in,
      setting up the tents
women bringing kindling and starting to cook
the wind blowing against the tent poles,
shaking the hides.
      Inside the bonfire and songs
            and smoke coming out of the tent . . .
Some ate buffalo meat brought from there.
and in his *trip** one saw another of an extinguished tribe.
and in their *trips** the Cheyenne saw the rivers of the sky
in psychedelic colors.
      And the Comanche sang
            We shall live again
            We shall live again
And the Caddo sang that they were already rising
            —and the Caddo were certainly rising!—
above, there where their people live, above,
                  where their people live
            Come, Caddo, let us all rise
                  Come, Caddo, let us all rise
      to the great Village
      to the great Village

Sitting Bull prophesized that
            the sacred feathers
would protect the Indians from nuclear fire.

By the Agency on Lake Walker, a ring as
in a circus

*In English in the original.

110

They waited all night long anxious to see Christ
At sunrise the crowd arrived, Christ
came with them. After breakfast Christ spoke to them.
        "I saw a scar on his face and another on his wrist
                I could not see his feet"
The last that was known of Wowoka:
he was seen at a fair in San Francisco.
The Dance went on, yet with a new hope
not immediate, feverish and delirious as before but
                a serene hope
like the hope for resurrection of the Christian
                according to Mooney.

And that great old man I saw in Taos
(with his gown and braids he seemed an old woman)
understood me when I said: *to heaven.**
Because the rickety *New England** tourist asked him
if he had known the buffalo: Yes, as a child;
                                and with sadness:
No more buffalo . . . *I wonder where they have GONE**
and I said *to heaven**
and the rickety tourist haha laughed as if it were a joke
and the old chief smiled sadly (and understood me)
(fall 1965, my trip to the usa to see
                Merton and the indians).

*In English in the original.

GLOSSARY

Achiote: The heart-leaved bixa or abotta.

Ahau: Each katun (i.e., period of 7200 years), according to the Mayan calendar, was named for the day (Ahau) in which it ended.

Ah Xupan: An early Mayan prophet.

Amate: Fig tree with milky juice.

Anahuac: Central plateau of Mexico; in Nahuatl: the earth.

Ave zacuan: Bird of warm regions, very destructive to the crops.

Ayllu: Each of the parcels of land into which the Inca community was divided.

Ayote: Gourd, squash.

Bejuco: Large creeping or climbing plant; rattan.

Cenote: Natural well.

Chac: Rain god of the Mayas.

Chachalaca: A bird, almost as large as a chicken; its meat is tasty and it screams constantly while it flies.

Chapulin: Grasshopper; also, a small child.

Chicha: Popular fermented beverage variously made from corn, pineapple, etc.

Chichen Itza: Mayan ruins in Yucatan, Mexico.

Chilamate: Large tree; cattle and wildlife feed on its fruits.

Chilam Balam: The books of Chilam Balam are the sacred books of the Maya of Yucatan. They were named after their last and greatest prophet, the Chilam from Chumayel.

Chilan: Prophet (also: chilam).

Chinampas: Intensely cultivated and watered garden plots.

Chumayel: Name of a village in the district of Tekax.

Cocom: Originally the most powerful family in Yucatan; it continued to exert power after the destruction of Mayapan.

Copal: The gum or resin of the copal was the principal incense used by the Mayas.

Copan: Ruins of the Classical Period in Guatemala.

Cuceb: Squirrel; in the Chilam Balam of Mani, the predictions for the twenty years of the Katun 5 Ahau were given this title.

Elote: Young corncob.

Guano: Seabird's dung, which is used as a fertilizer.

Huehuetl: A musical instrument.

Huitzilopochtli: Chief God of the Aztecs, the god of war. Human sacrifices were offered to him. He was also the Sun and it was believed that he was born every morning from the womb of Coatlicue, the goddess of the earth.

Hunaac Ceel: Ruler of Mayapan. He organized a conspiracy against Chichen Itza and conquered the city.

Katun: A measure of time which consisted of 20 tuns of 360 days each. Time was circular, and the same katun recurred after approximately 256 years.

Kukulkan: The Quetzalcoatl (or plumed serpent) of the Mayas.

Lapa: Bird of the tropical forests, with a long tail and
colorful plumage. Also called guacamayo.

Macehual: Commoners in the Mayan class system. Nobles were
called almehen.
Mata-palo: Tree which yields rubber and a fiber for sackcloth.
Mayapan: Civil capital of the Mayas under the Cocom family.
Milpa: Corn plot or field. The Mayas used the scorched
earth method for growing crops.

Netzahualcoyotl: Poet-philosopher ruler of the Chichimec
kingdom.
Nocheztli: Seed obtained from the nopal.

Ocote: Coniferous tree found in Mexico; its wood is used to
make torches.

Palenque: Ruins of the Classical Period of the Mayas in the
State of Chiapas, Mexico.
Peten: Region in Northern Guatemala where the Mayan ruins
of Uaxactun, Tikal, and Piedras Negras are found.
Pochote: Ceiba schottii.

Quetzal: National bird of Guatemala and sacred bird of the
Mayas. Also the name of the currency in Guatemala.
Quetzalcoatl: Aztec and Toltec God. Culture hero revered
for the introduction of learning and art; he was con-
sidered the essence of life on earth. He demanded
sacrifices only of butterflies and snakes.

Sol: The sun; also the name of the Peruvian currency.
Somoza: Name of a family of twentieth-century dictators in
Nicaragua.

Stela: Carved stone marking the periods of the Mayan calendar.

Tamoanchan: Probably the first civilized state in ancient
    Meso-America. In Mayan it means: Land of the Bird-Snake
    (or Feathered Serpent).
Tecolote: Owl.
Tejotli: Blue earth which is finely ground and used to
    paint gourds.
Teponaztli: Two-tongued drum, usually intricately carved.
Tikal: Mayan ruins in the Peten region.
Tizatl: Nahuatl for chalk.
Tlaloc: Rain god of the Aztecs.
Tlamatinimes: Wise men.
Tlilli: also tliltic, Nahuatl for: something black.
Tun: Each of the periods of 360 days, which formed a katun,
    in the Mayan calendar.

Uaxactun: Mayan ruins in the Peten region.
Usumacinta: River that serves as a border between Mexico
    and Guatemala.

Xiquipil: Unit used to count corn.

Yaravi: Indian tune.
Yaxchilan: Mayan ruins in the state of Chiapas, Mexico.

Zacate: Herb, grass, also used for forage.
Zapote: Tree that yields chicle; it has a plum-like fruit.
Zenzontle: Ash-colored bird.

THE JOHNS HOPKINS UNIVERSITY PRESS

This book was composed in Aldine Roman text and Garamond Light display
by Jones Composition Company, Inc., from a design by Laurie Jewell.
It was printed on Danforth, natural white, smooth finish, and bound in
Columbia Bayside Linen by The Maple Press Company.

Library of Congress Cataloging in Publication Data

Cardenal, Ernesto.
  Homage to the American Indians.

  Poems.
  1. Indians—Poetry. I. Title.
PQ7519.C34H613   861   73-8111
ISBN 0-8018-1513-4
ISBN 0-8018-1514-2 (pbk.)